RIO GRANDE DRAWDOWN

Tom's gaze fixed on the three horsemen, seated on their mounts in front of the hitch rail. The man in the middle caught his attention—a barrel-chested Mexican with crisscrossed bandoleers hanging from his shoulders and a pair of pistols tied to his waist.

"You have my horse!" a voice shouted, and now Tom knew the man wearing the bandoleers was Luis Valdez.

"He's mine now," Tom replied hoarsely, his hand moving closer to the butt of his .44.

"I give you a chance, *Tejano!* Give me back my horse or I will claim your life!"

"May not be quite that easy," Tom said, keeping his voice low. "I'm faster. You've got my word . . . you'll be the first to die."

The Mexican's grin faded. His lathered brown gelding stamped impatiently at a fly. It was the distraction Valdez had been waiting for.

His right hand clawed for his gun.

LAW OF THE GUN

FREDERIC BEAN

ZEBRA BOOKS
KENSINGTON PUBLISHING CORP.

ZEBRA BOOKS are published by

Kensington Publishing Corp.
475 Park Avenue South
New York, NY 10016

Zebra and the Z logo are trademarks of Kensington Publishing Corp.

First Printing: August, 1993

Printed in the United States of America

Chapter One

Tom Culpepper pushed up from his sagging hide-bottom chair and walked out on the front porch. A bottle of Kentucky bourbon dangled from his left fist, half its contents missing now, for it was past three in the afternoon. A blistering south Texas sun baked the pale caliche flats below the house, creating heat waves. Distorted images danced before Tom's eyes, a sight he'd grown accustomed to over the years, learning to compensate for the illusion when real movement occurred. There was a difference. When a horse and rider crossed the dry flats, even at a mile or more, he recognized it. Tom had always been a hard man to fool, as others would attest.

A horned lizard scurried across the hardpan below the porch. Tom called it his front yard, and though no grass grew, he insisted on having it attended. The old Mexican woman swept it every day with her broom, to make it more presentable should guests arrive. It was the prettiest stretch of caliche dirt in all of Texas, Rosa would say when her sweeping was done. And the cleanest.

Tom raised the bottle to his sun-cracked lips and took

a long, bubbling swallow. Then, as was his habit, he drew his sleeve across his mouth and gave a contented sigh. A gust of hot wind carried the sound away, so that at a distance, only his lips moved. Squinting in the sun's glare, he watched a dust devil swirl up from the riverbank, a tiny tornado full of dust that danced and wavered, changing direction, gaining intensity, then vanishing altogether.

Off in the distance, a burro brayed. Tom shook his head, for he knew it was old Pedro's burro and the animal was always hungry. So were Pedro's five children, and his rawboned wife, Carmen. It wasn't entirely Pedro's fault that his family went hungry most of the time. There wasn't much to eat in Rio Blanco, even in the best of times.

Tom's gaze drifted toward town. White adobe walls reflected sunlight with blinding brilliance off the cantina, and the *mercado*. It was early and the cantina was empty of patrons, thus there was no reason to walk down. Not yet. Arturo would be mopping the floor and the place would smell of lye.

Wind tossled Tom's mane of red and gray curls, lifting strands that touched his shoulders, sweeping a lock across one pale gray eye. He brushed the stray lock away with the back of his hand and then drank again. His leathery face puckered slightly when he felt the whiskey burn down his throat. Crow's feet webbed around his eyes, then relaxed.

"It's damn sure hot," he said, to himself, for he had no audience at the moment besides the dog. Hearing a human voice, the spotted dog resting in the shade at one end of the porch thumped its tail and lifted its nose toward Tom, blinking sleepily, passing its tongue over the soft folds of its upper lip expectantly, as if the voice meant food.

"It ain't time to eat yet," Tom said, when he saw the dog lick its chops. "Besides, tonight you'll have to get off your lazy ass an' go catch your own supper. I gave you all there was yesterday, you worthless bastard. Time you earned your own way 'round here."

The dog thumped its tail with renewed vigor while Tom spoke, as though the man had been praising it.

Tom made a face. "You ain't even smart enough to know when you've been cussed," he said. "Sorriest damn dog I ever owned. Worthless as teats on a boar."

He took his eyes off the dog and watched the cantina again. With nothing better to do, he turned back inside and removed his flat brim hat from a peg on the wall and stepped off the porch for a visit with Arturo. His high-heeled boots made a clumping sound as he started the short walk toward the cantina. The whiskey sloshed softly in his bottle when he lengthened his strides to hurry through the heat. A handful of chickens scattered from the roadway when his shadow fell across the ground, clucking angrily over his intrusion. Tom ignored the hens, thinking only of the cool interior of the adobe, even if the place did smell of lye. Farther down the street, he glimpsed a woman's skirt in the doorway of the *mercado*. Who would be at the market this time of day, he wondered?

As he predicted he would, he scented the damp soapy smell of Arturo's mop when he neared the cantina and he heard the scrape of a wooden bucket across the floor.

"Damn fool's gonna mop all the way down to bedrock," he mumbled, pausing at the open door frame to allow his eyes to adjust to the bad light.

7

A balding Mexican looked up from his work, standing in a circle of filmy water with a mop handle in both hands. "Ah, it is you," he said, motioning Tom inside. "Consuelo is in the back."

"I'm not lookin' for the whore," Tom replied gruffly, stepping around the clean spot on the floor. "Wasn't interested in that. Too hot just now."

Arturo nodded without looking up. "*Sí*, it is too hot for most things," he said wearily.

Tom saw a figure behind the bar, wiping a rag over rows of clean glasses. He wished Consuelo hadn't been there right then. It had been almost a week since he buck-jumped her and he'd planned to make it another week before he gave in to urges.

Consuelo turned and looked at him, and it seemed her face had grown rounder. Framed by ringlets of black hair, her cheeks looked plump, puffy. Wearing a low-fronted cotton blouse, her big breasts were squeezed together, half spilling over the top, quivering like mounds of egg custard when she moved her arms to wipe off the glasses.

"How come you don't want me?" she asked in a pouty voice, her eyes narrowing. "I heard what you say to Arturo."

"Too hot," Tom replied, walking to a window for fresh air, and to avoid Consuelo's stare.

"It is always hot in Rio Blanco," she remarked, tinkling glass behind Tom's back. "Maybe you get too old to need a woman, Tom."

"I ain't too old," he grumbled, looking out the window at nothing in particular. "It's just too goddamn hot, is all."

"Maybe," Consuelo said, her tone hinting of doubt.

8

"Or maybe you have become *un viejo* . . . like an old man."

Her persistence had begun to rankle him. "You've let yourself get fat, Consuelo," he said. "You ain't as pretty as you used to be."

A glass banged heavily behind him. *"Bastardo,"* she snapped.

A slow grin lifted the corners of his mouth. Maybe now the woman would be quiet and leave him alone.

"And you have let yourself get old, Tom," Consuelo fired back. "Too old to make a woman happy!"

This kind of banter wasn't what he wanted. He turned away from the window. "Maybe if I found a woman that wasn't too goddamn fat, I'd work harder at it," he said, starting for the door.

Consuelo's face was a mask of hatred. "Then go find a skinny *puta,* old man!" she shouted, placing her hands on her ample hips. "You will come begging before I ever open my legs for you again!"

Tom shrugged and walked through the doorway, blinking in bright sunlight, glad to be free of the lye smell and the insults of Rio Blanco's fat whore. Were there just one more whore in town, he would swear off Consuelo for good this time. He wasn't getting old at all. Consuelo had gotten fat, plain and simple.

Arturo came out behind Tom to empty his bucket in the road. Tom glanced at the smelly contents of the bucket. "Better get a decent *puta* or you'll go broke," he said. "I ain't gonna waste no more of my money on a fat woman."

Arturo sighed and shook his head. "But where, señor? Who will come to Rio Blanco any more? I am already broke, because no one comes to this place."

Tom was sure he understood. "It's that fat whore, drivin' off all your business."

Arturo gazed blankly across the brush below his cantina. "There is no business," he said softly, sadly. "Everyone has moved away, to places where there is rain."

Tom looked at the sky. "It'll rain again, one of these days, and then folks will come back. Can't stay dry more'n three years in a row."

Arturo's deep black eyes fell on Tom. "But it has. This will be four years now, and we have no rain."

Tom looked at the dry riverbed west of the *mercado*. It had been so long since there had even been a muddy trickle in the Rio Blanco that he'd forgotten what it looked like. He counted the years and wondered if Arturo could be right. Had it been four years since the last measurable rain? "It ain't been quite that long," he said after a thoughtful pause. "More like two and a half years."

Arturo wanted no part of the argument. He tossed out the milky water in his bucket and turned for the door.

"Maybe it has been three years," Tom added, frowning.

"It is four," the old man whispered hoarsely, as if saying it aloud might somehow worsen things. He hobbled inside the cantina with his bucket, leaving Tom alone with his thoughts.

"Can't be," he said under his breath. "Arturo can't count."

Or could he? Had it been four years? Looking around at what was left of the town, the empty adobes crumbling with neglect and the dry, barren flats around Rio Blanco where grass once grew, it was entirely possible that four years had gone by. Half the people who used

10

to live here had moved on, but they'd done it slowly, a few families each year, making the exodus less noticeable. Someone said that less than thirty people lived here now, someone with nothing better to do than to count heads. It didn't seem possible, that only thirty folks remained. Less than thirty, according to the unofficial census taker.

"Damn," Tom whispered, gazing across the rooftops from the front porch of the cantina. "This place is liable to be a ghost town if it don't rain mighty soon."

It was an inescapable fact that the cattle herds had shrunk in the last couple of years, but that was due to a lack of water. Only the spring-fed hole remained at a bend in the riverbed five miles southwest of town, to water livestock. It was a shrinking water hole since last summer and everyone worried that the spring was drying up. Cattlemen blamed *los borregos,* the sheep, for causing the pool to shrink. Hank Wardlaw swore that sheep packed down the caliche with their sharp little hooves and that caused the spring to close up at the bottom of the pool. Hank didn't raise any sheep . . . he'd have rather been seen naked at church than own *borregos,* so it was natural enough that a cattleman would blame something else.

Tom had thinned his own cattle herd by more than half, and the cows he had left were starving. Cattle buyers from San Antonio wouldn't buy cows that were mostly skin and bones, leaving Rio Blanco cattlemen without a market for the calves they produced. Things had gotten so bad that ranchers ignored property lines and allowed the mixed herds to graze together, wherever there was scant grass. And all the herds needed the water from the river bend pool, as did the sheep and goat

11

herders. There wasn't any room for argument over it. No one wanted to see animals perish.

Tom took a deep breath, then a swallow of whiskey. For the last twenty years, he had called Rio Blanco home, even served briefly as its sheriff, back when there was a town council, and enough businessmen to pay his wages. But as the years became drier, so did the city treasury, and now the town was without a sheriff. Just two business establishments remained, the cantina and the market, and both were failing because of the drought.

"I always liked it here," he said softly, remembering better times when Rio Blanco was full of celebrating cowboys on payday, and drummers peddling their wares to a mercantile, Roy Baker's big mercantile that was now closed, just down the street. Roy and his family had moved on in '89, to escape the poverty when folks had no money to buy his wares. Nobody could blame Roy for leaving. There had been others, a blacksmith named Rogers who stayed just one year and nearly starved to death, the Villareal family who operated the little cafe and bakery since the town was founded back in '68. When it didn't rain, folks couldn't afford baked goods any longer, or meals eaten away from home.

"I'm too old to start over again someplace else," he said, saying it very quietly, so Consuelo couldn't hear his admission. He was fifty-four, still young enough for some things, too old for others, like moving on to start another cattle herd where pastures were green. He wouldn't have the money to start over anyway. Cattle buyers would not offer him anything for his rangy long-horn mother cows, and his fall calves from last year were stunted from lack of nourishment. There wouldn't

12

be enough beef on his calves to interest a cattle buyer until it rained.

Off to the west, he saw a dust cloud moving toward Rio Blanco and he guessed it would be the Wardlaw boys, and the cattle buyer who came down yesterday from San Antone. Hank had announced that he meant to sell out, if he could, to the highest bidder. Only one interested buyer had answered his letter and come down to make an offer on the Wardlaw herd.

Four riders approached the riverbank, Hank and his son, old Jessie Kootz, and a stranger in a derby hat. Tom watched the stranger trot his horse down to the dry riverbed, thinking. "He didn't offer much," Tom assured himself. "Maybe five dollars a head for the young stock."

He took a drink of whiskey and leaned back against the wall of the cantina to await the arrival of Wardlaw, and the grim news Tom knew he would bring, the buyer's offer. Dust rolled away from the trotting horses in great, billowy clouds, swept east by the ever-present hot wind.

Hank Wardlaw said all he needed to say before he halted his horse in front of the cantina. His face mirrored his bad humor over the offer that had been made for his cows. Past fifty, Hank had seen too much sun and wind in his lifetime. He cheeks were like dried cowhide and it seemed he wore a perpetual sour expression.

"Howdy, Tom," Hank said, swinging down from his weathered, high-backed saddle. His shirt and denims were layered with caliche chalk that had turned to mud where sweat soaked through. His gray hat was sweat-stained, greasy where his hands touched the brim and crown. He looped his reins over the rail and waited for the man in the derby to reach the ground.

Tom acknowledged Hank's greeting with a nod. Jessie, almost seventy years of age and crippled by rheumatism, eased his right leg painfully over the rump of his horse and stepped down before Bob, youngest of Hank Wardlaw's sons, could dismount. But Tom's attention was on the cattle buyer from San Antonio in his brown vested suit and derby hat, all of which was now coated with caliche. The man had muttonchop sideburns and nervous blue eyes Tom didn't like. Tom knew this man couldn't be trusted.

"Mr. Burke," Hank began, "want you to meet Rio Blanco's most famous citizen. This here's none other than T.C. Culpepper, the gunfighter. We call him Tom, 'cause that's his rightful name. Tom, shake hands with Mr. Wayland Burke from San Antone."

The cattle buyer gave Tom a surprised look. He reached for his derby and took it off, before offering his hand to shake with Tom. "Why, I've heard about you all my life, Mr. Culpepper," he said. "Had no idea you lived here. It's fair to say that folks all over the state know about you, sir. Like Hank says, you're a downright famous feller. Back in those days, you outgunned every bad hombre there was, didn't you?"

Tom took Burke's fleshy hand, then let it drop quickly, disliking the soft feel of it. "That was a long time ago," he said, which was his usual answer when someone mentioned his past, before he came to Rio Blanco.

"I see you're still carryin' a gun," Burke said, dropping his gaze to Tom's gunbelt. "I reckon, this close to the Mexican border, you still get a chance to use a gun now and then."

"It's been a while," Tom answered, which was the truth. It had been a very long while, better than a dozen years if he remembered correctly, and that time it had only been needed to convince a rowdy drunk to keep quiet inside the cantina.

"Well, sir, it's a pleasure to make your acquaintance, Mr. Culpepper," Burke said, grinning. "I'll have a story to tell when I get back to the office, about meeting one of the most famous old-timers in the whole state of Texas."

Tom bristled. A fifty-four-year-old man was hardly an old-timer, though he might be considered a bit long in the tooth for a man who used to make his living with a gun. Few gunmen lived long lives back when the border country was lawless. "I'm not ready for a rocking chair quite yet," he said coldly, offended by Burke's remark, trying not to show it too plainly.

"I'm sellin' my herd, Tom," Hank said, ending Tom's annoyance over a reference to his age.

"What'sa cow worth these days?" Tom asked, directing the question to the cattle buyer. "I may have a few head I want to sell, if the price suits me."

Burke's cheeks colored. "Not much, I'm afraid," he said, with a sideways glance at Hank. "Not for half-starved longhorns. Most cattle these days are mixed breed. Hereford crosses, so the calves will have more beef. Not much demand for a longhorn now. They're outdated. A part of the past, maybe like the old time gunfighters you used to outdraw, back when things were wild."

It had begun to seem that Burke meant serious offense directed at Tom, with all this talk about out-of-date things. Tom stiffened and fixed the cattle buyer with a steely look. "First off, you didn't answer my question about what a cow's worth, mister," he said, an edge to his voice that was unmistakable. "And I'm startin' to resent the way you're talkin' about longhorns and shootists, so before I get mad and put a bullet hole through that fancy suit you're wearin', I'll go someplace else. A longhorn's still the toughest creature on this earth, mister, and I'm still quick enough with a .44 to blow a hole in your belly before you can scratch your damned ear. Never mind what you're payin' for cattle . . . I wouldn't sell my cows to the likes of you if you was payin' a hundred dollars a head!"

With that said, Tom turned on his heel and stalked off toward his house. His boots crunched across the dry caliche, the only sound after Tom's heated speech in front of the cantina. With his jaw set, Tom marched to his front porch and climbed the pair of sagging steps to go inside. Just as he reached the front door, he swung a look back at the four men beside the hitch rail. Wayland Burke stood in front of Hank with his palms spread, trying to explain something Tom couldn't hear.

Tom knew damn well what the cattle buyer was saying to the Wardlaw cowboys . . . he was trying to talk his way out of a fix that had almost gotten him killed.

Chapter Two

He was decidedly drunk and he knew it. The floor had tilted in a crazy fashion when he got up to let the Flores girl in with his clean laundry.

"Put it in the bedroom," he said, holding on to the door frame for support while Maria padded barefoot across the floor, walking between Tom and the lantern burning softly on a table beside the bedroom door. "Hang them shirts up so they won't wrinkle. Took your mama a long time to iron 'em up nice, so be careful."

When Maria passed the lantern, her thin dress admitted enough light so he caught a glimpse of her body, just the outline of it.

"By God, Maria, you're gettin' bumps on your chest, ain't you?" he asked, feeling the whiskey wash around inside his skull while he steadied himself against the door. "How old are you now, Maria?"

Before she disappeared into the dark bedroom she flashed him a smile, a pretty smile full of even white teeth. "Sixteen, Señor Tom," she giggled. "And they are much more than bumps. Very soon they will be as big as Consuelo's. Mama told me."

Tom shook his head. Little Maria had grown up all of a sudden and he'd hardly noticed. "You're gettin' mighty pretty," he said, loud enough so she could hear him in the bedroom. "You say they're already bigger than little bumps? Well I'll declare! Hadn't noticed they was so big. Mighty interestin' news, Maria. Mighty interestin' to know they're growin' so fast."

She appeared at the bedroom door smiling broadly, with her chest thrust forward to show the outline of her breasts through her shapeless homespun dress. "See how big they are?" she asked playfully, posing for him in the lantern light.

"I'll be damned," he said softly, eyes fastened to the twin mounds she was showing him. "Big as a man's fist, they are. You're a full-grown woman now, ain't you?"

"Almost," she replied, teasing him with a slight turn that gave him a side view of the curve of her breasts. "They grow bigger when I sleep. When I wake up in the morning, I can see how much bigger they are."

He took his eyes off her chest to examine her face. In the lamplight, she was a pretty young Mexican girl and he hadn't even noticed it until now. "Hellfire, Maria, you'll be marryin' age right soon. Havin' babies all over the place."

Maria's smile faded. "No, no, Señor Tom," she said darkly, pinching her brow. "I will not marry and have *niños* like my mother. I will become a beautiful *puta*, more beautiful than Consuelo when she first came to Rio Blanco. I will make the *vaqueros* pay me to open my legs for them when I go to another town to become a *puta*."

Tom scowled. "Why on earth would you want to be a whore?" he asked softly.

Maria lifted her chin. "Because the *putas* of Laredo wear pretty satin dresses and silk ribbons in their hair. They have shoes with high heels, and silk stockings. They are not poor, like a woman who has babies and a husband. I am tired of being poor, Señor Tom."

Tom's scowl deepened. "Bein' a whore ain't such a good idea," he said, preparing a list of reasons against it. "Everybody'll treat you different, like you was trash. Won't nobody want you to go to church with 'em, or go to nice places. Look at Consuelo. Every cowboy within twenty miles of here cusses her and treats her like she was dirt. Which she is, I reckon. And there's all kinds of diseases a whore's liable to get, like the Pox. You're too pretty to be a whore, Maria. You oughta think about doin' something else with yourself."

She shook her head side to side. "My mind is made up," she said flatly. "When I have saved enough money, I will go to Laredo or San Antonio to become a *puta*. But don't tell my mother or my father about it, Señor Tom. Please! It will be a secret between us. I only told you because you noticed how big my bosoms are. *Vaqueros* like big bosoms. Consuelo told me."

"That fat bitch oughta learn to keep her mouth shut about things like that," he snapped. "She's got no business saying things like that to a child!"

"I am not a child," Maria protested. "See?" Unexpectedly, she lifted the hem of her dress, all the way to the tops of her breasts, revealing that underneath, she was naked. "Look at my body, Señor Tom, and you will know that I am not a child any longer. I am a woman now!"

He closed his eyes briefly when he glimpsed a mound of dark hair at the tops of Maria's thighs. "Cover yourself," he scolded softly, opening his eyes again before her dress fell to her knees. "I can see that you're a woman under there. But that ain't all there is to bein' full growed. There's other things."

She skipped across the room to the door frame where Tom stood, then she stood on her tiptoes to kiss his cheek. "Remember," she whispered. "It is a secret that I plan to leave Rio Blanco. Please do not tell anyone. Perhaps, before I leave, I will come to your house in the dark and prove to you that I am a woman. You still think of me as a silly little girl, but I know many things about being a woman. Consuelo showed me many things about pleasing a man. *Buenas noches,* Señor Tom."

She was out the door and running away from the porch before his whiskey-ridden brain could think of more arguments against her idea. He swung around the door frame, holding on with one hand, to watch the girl disappear into the darkness.

"It's that fat whore's doing," he said later, when his mind would work. "Consuelo has talked that little girl into selling herself. Somebody oughta knock some sense into Consuelo's skull a'fore she ruins Maria. Damn that fat bitch anyway, it ain't none of her affair!"

His vision was fuzzy when he left the front door for another drink of whiskey, and his feet didn't obey his commands properly when he made his way toward the bottle on the kitchen table. It was his second bottle of the day, he remembered. He'd gotten drunk, to get over being mad about the remarks the cattle buyer made, about Tom being an old-timer, and out-of-date longhorns not being worth much. While it was true that he had once made a living with a gun, that fact did not mark him as useless now. Across the Rio Grande, barely twenty-five miles to the south, there were still plenty of border bandits and dangerous pistoleros who needed the sting of a bullet now and then to remind them to leave Texas cattle and horses alone. And as to a longhorn cow, they were the only breed of cattle tough enough to survive a dry south Texas desert like the land around Rio Blanco. A Hereford would have starved to death the first year of the drought they were in now. Hadn't Warren Cobb given Herefords a try? Back in '84, when both of his high-priced Hereford bulls died of thirst trying to make it to the water hole at Rio Blanco bend?

Tom hoisted the bottle to his mouth and drank deeply. What did that fancy-suited bastard from San Antonio know about raising cows in south Texas? He'd have gone out of business the first year, like Warren Cobb, if he tried to raise Herefords down here.

"To hell with Wayland Burke," he said, then he drank again.

Somewhere off in the darkness, a burro brayed.

"I wish Pedro would feed that jackass," Tom complained, gazing out a kitchen window. He was silent a moment longer. "I wonder what ol' Pedro would think if he knowed his daughter aims to become a goddamn whore. He's got that fat bitch Consuelo to thank for that! Ain't nothin' more useless than a fat whore with a big mouth on her."

Then he remembered the sight of Maria's naked body. "Damn if she hasn't growed up all of a sudden," he said. A soft night wind fluttered the curtains beside the window, curtains sewn from flour sacking which Rosa made. They gave the house a woman's touch, for reasons

21

Rosa never bothered to explain. No man in his right mind wanted fluffy white curtains with little blue flowers on them, but he'd been unable to persuade Rosa to leave the windows the way they were. What did a fifty-four-year-old bachelor care about the way a place looked?

Later, he clumped over to the lantern and extinguished it on his way to bed, still reeling drunk, still thinking about Maria and her ripe young breasts. He sat on the bed and pulled off his boots, then his bib front shirt and faded denims. A cool westerly breeze blew through the bedroom windows. He lay back and stared at the dark before he drifted off to sleep. His final conscious thought was one of anger. Just who did that cattle buyer think he was, calling Tom an old-timer?

His head was throbbing while he worked the pump jack behind the house. Morning sunlight turned the surrounding brushland a golden color, though his head hurt too terribly to notice such things at the moment. He worked the pump and muttered under his breath, for the water would not rise. Of late, most of the wells in Rio Blanco gave water reluctantly. Juan Diaz said the water level was dropping due to the drought, which made sense, since everything else around Rio Blanco was going down, especially cattle prices.

Across town, goats and sheep bleated from crowded corrals and the sound grew to a chorus. And predictably, Pedro Flores's burro brayed. Then, as an unwanted distraction that took Tom's attention from the pump, his high-withered bay gelding stuck its head over the corral fence and nickered for its breakfast corn.

Tom looked up and pulled a sour face when he heard

22

the horse. "Is every goddamn thing in this town hungry?" he asked, giving the gelding a baleful stare. "Can't you see I'm tryin' to get some damn water here?"

An added irritation arrived in the form of the spotted dog. It came up behind Tom and licked the back of his bare leg affectionately, wagging its tail furiously while greeting its master. The wet tongue came unexpectedly and Tom jumped when he felt something against his calf. "Son of a bitch!" he cried, whirling around to see if a rattlesnake had bitten him while he was half asleep.

The dog whimpered, staring up at Tom with big liquid eyes, its tail thrashing back and forth happily when it heard Tom's voice.

Tom saw the dog and his shoulders sagged. "It's you," he said, sounding disgusted. He loved the old dog, as much as a man can love an animal, but it was a well-kept secret around Rio Blanco. Tom cussed the dog at the top of his lungs, mostly for being too lazy to go off hunting, or whatever else happened to displease Tom at the moment. The dog had grown so accustomed to its master's angry tone that it actually welcomed it.

"Don't ever do that again!" Tom shouted, feeling the pain worsen in his skull when he raised his voice. He shook his finger at the dog and turned back to the pump, for there still was no water in the wash pan and it seemed to Tom that he'd been pumping for an eternity. "Goddamn dog's gonna give me a rupture one of these days," he mumbled unhappily, working the pump handle again. He had come out to the well in his underwear the way he did every morning, going unnoticed usually. But the cussing he'd given the dog and his horse brought Delia

Cummings out on her back porch across the way, to see what the ruckus was about.

He saw her from the corner of his eye. "Mornin', Miz Cummings," he said, speaking matter-of-factly, as though he often walked about half naked.

"Mornin', Tom," Delia replied. "You forgot to get dressed this morning. Sign of old age, when a man forgets to wear his pants."

Tom halted the pump handle and tossed the wash basin to the ground. "I wish to hell everybody'd stop tellin' me how old I'm gettin'," he growled, shaking his head even though it pained him to do so. "It's got to where a man can't even have a minute of privacy in this dried-up town. This fall, when it gets cool enough to dig the post holes, I'm gonna build a solid fence across my backyard, so I can come out plumb naked if I take the notion."

Delia frowned. "I wouldn't do that if I were you, Tom," she said. "Somebody's liable to think you've gone loco. An' besides, your legs look like bleached cattle bones. I'd wear britches, so folks wouldn't snicker at my legs."

Tom let out an impatient sigh. "Go right ahead and snicker at my legs, Miz Cummings. I ain't gonna get all dressed up in my Sunday best just so's I can come after a pan of water."

Delia turned to go back inside her house. "Don't appear you're havin' much luck gettin' the water, Tom. That well's goin' dry, same as ours." She opened her back door, then she hesitated and gave Tom a wry grin. "Come to think of it, that's the first time I ever remember seein' you without your gunbelt, Tom. There's some

-24-

in this town who have speculated that you sleep with it on.''

She went inside before he could offer argument. He faced the pump again and took a deep breath. ''Nosiest goddamn place on earth,'' he said. ''I'm gonna build that goddamn fence this fall. I'm damn sure gonna get it built.''

A tiny spit of rust-colored water dribbled from the mouth of the pump. Then, after a few more strokes, he got enough water to shave and take a standing bath. When he picked up the wash pan, he saw a red rooster belonging to Benito Sanchez lift its tail feathers and deposit a glistening pile of droppings squarely in the middle of his backyard.

Tom swung an angry look at the dog. ''A hound that won't bark when a chicken shits in the yard is plumb worthless,'' he snapped, climbing his back porch with the wash pan.

The dog wagged its tail and licked its lips, watching its master, completely ignoring the rooster.

He shaved and dressed, combing his thick red hair before he strapped on his gun and went to the wood stove. Tossing a few knots of mesquite into the belly, he struck a match and blew flames to life before closing the door. Soon the heavy cast-iron skillet was sizzling yesterday's bacon grease. He cut strips of salt pork and set them in to fry. Later, he broke two eggs beside the bacon and stared glumly at his breakfast. He'd been without coffee beans for a week because the mercado was out of them and the freight wagon from Laredo wouldn't be in Rio Blanco until next Tuesday.

''Breakfast without coffee is near 'bout as bad as crawlin' between a fat woman's thighs,'' he grumbled.

25

Last night, he had vague dreams about Consuelo and pretty little Maria, although in his dream, Maria had gotten fat, just like Consuelo, so that he had trouble telling the two women apart.

Off in the distance, he heard a running horse. It was unusual for anyone to be galloping a horse around Rio Blanco in the morning, unless there was some kind of trouble.

He tossed his fork aside and walked to the front door, where he heard the sounds growing louder. When he came out on the porch, he saw a rider hurrying toward town beneath a cloud of dust.

"Something's wrong," he told himself. "A man don't run a horse like that in this heat unless something's wrong."

When the rider drew near, Tom recognized him, a boy named Jesus Soto who punched cattle for Chap Grant south of town. Chap owned the west bank of the Rio Blanco around the spring pool, and ran more cattle than the other ranchers as a result. Jesus was using his horse hard to reach town and Tom knew it spelled trouble.

Jesus jerked his lathered sorrel to a halt in front of Tom's house, and began to speak in a loud voice before the dust settled.

"A bunch of cows have been stolen, Señor Tom!" the boy cried.

"Stolen?" Tom had trouble believing his ears.

"*Sí.* We followed the tracks all the way to the border early this morning. Thirty-one cows, and the calves!"

Tom frowned. "Where did they cross, Jesus?"

"At the Flat Rock crossing . . . you know the place?"

"Sure, I know it. It's shallow there, and there are quicksand beds on both sides."

"Señor Chap, he says to find you, and to tell you to come quick," Jesus panted, his youthful face glistening with sweat beneath the brim of his wide sombrero. "Some of the missing cows are yours, Señor Tom. We have lost eighteen, and the rest belong to you!"

Tom's hands closed involuntarily, making fists. "I'll saddle my horse and get my rifle. How many men were driving the herd?"

"We found the tracks of four horses, but now the cattle are safe in Mexico, señor."

Tom shook his head. "Ain't nothin' of mine safe in Mexico when it's been stolen," he snarled. "I'll ride across that river and get those cattle back. Just give me time to get my horse."

Chapter Three

He rode beside Chap Grant until they reached the banks of the Rio Grande. Chap didn't have much to say, and Tom guessed his silence was concern that his losses might wipe him out this year. Like all the other ranchers in the area, Chap was barely holding on during the drought and the loss of eighteen cows and calves might be just enough to push Chap over the edge. He owed the bank in Laredo for feed that got him through last winter and without calves to sell, even cheap calves, Chap couldn't pay his bank loan.

Tom faced a similar dilemma. Thirteen of the missing cow-calf pairs were his, although he didn't owe a feed bill on them. Not yet, unless the drought lasted. Tom still had some saved money, not much, but enough to see him through for another year.

They halted their horses on a bluff above the river. Tom made a study of the tracks where the herd had entered the Rio Grande.

"Four men, just like Jesus said," he muttered. Then he looked across the river at Mexico. A few miles to the east of the crossing lay the Mexican village of Guerrero.

It had been an outlaw's roost twenty years earlier, one of the roughest border towns in all of northern Mexico, until times changed. Now there were Texas Ranger posts and military garrisons all along the Rio Grande, making life too dangerous for bandits and thieves crossing back and forth.

Chap ran a hand across his untrimmed beard, narrowing his eyes. In his middle forties, he was a product of the border country, the son of an early pioneer in south Texas and he knew his way around cattle and ranch work. "What'll we do, Tom?" he asked.

"Go after our goddamn cattle," Tom answered quickly. "Get every last one of 'em back."

"It's against the law."

Tom merely shrugged. "You know what it will be like to go through officials over yonder. They'll hem and haw, and do nothing while our cows are headed to Mexico City. It'll be a waste of time to make a report at Guerrero, Chap. You do whatever suits you, but I'm goin' across to get my cows back. Damn the sorry sons of bitches who'll steal a poor man's cows like this. They're common outlaws, and they deserve a shallow grave, or a good ass whipping. Either way, I'm gettin' my stock back."

"Could be dangerous, Tom," Chap said. "They're liable to have guns and put up a fight."

Tom nodded once. "Suits the hell outta me. Ain't had a good scrap with *pistoleros* in a few years. High time I gave my guns a good cleanin' anyways."

Chap was staring at him. "That was a while back, when you used to tangle with *bandidos*."

"Are you sayin' I ain't able to handle myself?" Tom asked.

"No, not exactly, Tom. But things have changed since then."

Tom's eyelids became slits. "One thing don't never change, and that's what a bullet does to a goddamn thief! I can still shoot as straight as I need to shoot. Ain't a goddamn thing wrong with my eyes, pardner."

Chap looked across the river again. "There could be trouble with the Federales if we ride over and start shootin' to get our cattle back. They might throw us in jail and we'd stay there until we went to rot."

Tom's cheeks hardened. "Never had you figured for a coward, Chap."

Chap's eyes wavered. "I ain't a coward, Tom. Times are different now. You used to do whatever you damn well pleased in this country, and nobody ever challenged you over it. But things ain't the same as they was back then. We could wind up in jail."

Tom had heard enough. He pulled his Colt .44 and thumbed open the loading gate to inspect the gleam of brass-jacketed cartridges in sunlight. "You can do whatever you want," he said quietly, "but I'm goin' over after my cows. To hell with the Federales and anybody else who gets in my way. Them longhorns are mine and I aim to get every last one of 'em back."

"I'd sure like to go," Chap began, although his voice lacked conviction. "Hell, Tom, I've got a wife and kids to think about. If I get tossed in a Mexican jail, I could be there the rest of my life. What would Sara do? And what about my girls?"

Tom jammed his pistol into its holster and lifted his reins from the bay's withers. "Do whatever suits you, Chap. I won't hold it against you if you elect to stay.

Keep an eye on the rest of my herd whilst I'm gone. I'll be back, with my cows and yours, if I'm able.''

Chap extended a gloved hand to shake with Tom. ''Be careful over there,'' he said. ''It ain't the same place it used to be. A few old thin-hided longhorns ain't worth dyin' for.''

Tom jutted his jaw and stared across the Rio Grande. ''That's your opinion on things, Chap. Me, I'd rather be in a six-foot hole than allow a bunch of Mexican cow rustlers to have the last word on things. I've killed a few men in my time, and my time ain't over just yet . . . contrary to what some others think. I can still use a gun, and I've goddamn sure still got my pride. The sorry sons of bitches who stole them cattle ain't got away with it yet. Be seein' you, Chap. Ask somebody to feed my ol' spotted dog while I'm away.''

Tom nudged his horse with a spur and started down to the crossing at a trot. The bay snorted when it came to the water and bowed its neck, until Tom rattled his spurs into the gelding's sides.

In late summer, and during a dry year, the Rio Grande hardly reached the bay's belly even in the deepest spots. Tom watched for sign of quicksand beds while the horse negotiated the river. In the back of his mind, though he never said outright, he had Chap pegged for a yellow coward. A man who wouldn't take some risks to get back his rightful property wasn't much of a rancher, in Tom's view.

He rode out on the far side and turned back in the saddle to see if Chap was watching. Chap waved from the bluff and reined his horse out of sight. Tom roweled the bay along the cattle tracks as a midafternoon sun slanted under his hat brim. The herd had been driven almost due south away from the river. Off in the distance he could see the outlines of rocky canyons against a cloudless sky. If he were any judge of outlaw behaviour, the rustlers would take the cows into the maze of empty canyons below Guerrero. Only someone who knew the country would be able to find a herd of longhorns hidden in those canyons. And if anyone knew the lay of things down there, it was Tom Culpepper.

He sent the horse to a short lope and settled against his saddle for the ride. It would be dark before he reached the most likely hiding places for a stolen herd, which suited his purposes. In the dark, one man could move about almost unnoticed in those canyons, if he knew what he was about, and stayed watchful.

He glanced down at his Winchester .44, resting in a saddle boot beneath his left leg. The rifle was chambered for the same shells as his pistol, a habit he developed back when things often happened too quickly for a leisurely selection of the proper caliber. And though he seldom indulged in recollections from his violent past, he did so now, briefly, to pass the time more than anything else. It was good, sometimes, to think back to those days. He didn't feel so useless back then. It had been a time when he had the respect of other men, because of his skill with a gun. Most everyone along the border knew him, if only by reputation. There was a certain satisfaction when he walked into a place and heard men whisper his name behind cupped hands, although he never kidded himself about the reason for his fame. Other men feared him. He was a paid killer, a gun for hire who left almost a score of dead men in his wake before he ended it. And he could truthfully claim that hardly a one of them didn't deserve to die, for one reason or another. Almost to a man, they had sought the chance to test their skill with a gun against him. And to the last man, they had all been too slow.

There was just that one killing that bothered him, the last man to die in front of Tom's gun. And that shooting had marked the end of it for Tom, and the beginning of a quieter life. Times, he still remembered the boy and it was always an unhappy recollection.

He sighed along the tracks, then the horizon, keeping the bay in a collected lope. He had promised himself a long time ago that the last man had fallen in front of his gun, if there was another way to settle it. But when a gang of brazen bandits tried to steal his livelihood, he would make an exception. If they gave him back the cattle quietly he would try to avoid a fight. The prospects for a peaceful settlement didn't seem likely, but he would make the try if the rustlers allowed it.

The sun lowered to the western hills, painting shadows below yucca plants and cholla. Now the air was cooler. His bay galloped easily, barely breaking a lather as the temperature lowered.

At the mouth of the first yawning canyon, the tracks turned sharply into the opening. ''Damn fools are gonna make it easy,'' he said, swinging beside the prints, watching the canyon rim in the fading light. ''Don't appear these gents are none too smart,'' he added softly. ''Maybe they're figurin' nobody'll come after 'em.''

He slowed the bay to a jog trot when he neared a pass through the canyon. A rifleman high in the rocks would have an easy time of ambushing a lone rider. Keeping the bay to stretches of shadow from the rim above, he rode into the pass at a trot. The bay's iron shoes echoed hollowly off the sheer rock faces on both sides, the only sound in a canyon blanketed by silence. It was dusky dark by the time he made it through the pass into a second canyon, and when he glimpsed what awaited him across the canyon floor, he jerked the gelding to a halt and frowned.

A herd of longhorns grazed peacefully on the far side of the canyon. He recognized the cows at once, a big spotted cow with a six-foot horn spread, and a slab-sided yellow dun cow that also bore his brand. And off to the left of the herd, sat a one-room clapboard cabin with a pole corral behind it encircling a slant roofed shed. A pair of muley horses rested hipshot inside the corral. A window of the shack glowed softly with lantern light.

"This is damn sure easy," he said under his breath. "Didn't even post a lookout along their back trail. Don't seem these boys have got much sense."

An old windmill fanned its wooden blades east of the corral. Tom could hear the sucker rod rattling up and down when a gust of wind blew past. He tied a knot in his reins so both hands would be free to use his guns, then he drew the Winchester and levered a shell into the chamber and rested the stock against his left knee. Urging the bay forward, he guided the horse with his legs and pulled his Colt revolver, cocking it, listening to the single-action ream click into place. He had never learned to trust double-action pistols even though some men insisted they fired faster. Tom's movements with a gun were practiced, sure, reflexive with the older model Colts and he wouldn't make the change.

When he approached the cabin, expecting the door to fly open at any moment, followed by a wall of gunfire, he grew puzzled. Even someone who was stone deaf would have heard his horse riding up, so why had no one come to the door? Looking at his surroundings, he wondered briefly if he were riding into a trap, but there was no cover for hidden gunmen around the cabin. So why were things so quiet?

A horse nickered from the corral. Tom's hands tensed around his guns, for he knew the sound would bring men pouring outside, men who feared trouble over a herd of stolen cattle. Yet still, as he rode closer, no one came out.

He was fifty yards from the front door when lantern light suddenly spilled from the doorway. A man's form was silhouetted in the square of light and Tom knew the shooting was about to begin.

"Quién es?" a voice asked. It was a youthful voice, a very young boy asking who was there. Tom could plainly see there was no gun in the young man's hands.

"Whoa," Tom said, and the bay halted. "Tom Culpepper, and I've come for them cows you stole from me. Now, step out here where I can see you, boy, or I'll blow a hole in you big enough to toss a tomcat through!"

The boy obeyed quickly, but Tom was not fooled. He aimed his Colt at the doorway into the cabin. "Tell the others to come out!" he shouted. He had the advantage, being out in the dark while whoever was inside would be blinded by the lantern.

"I am alone, señor," the boy stammered, speaking thickly accented English. "The others . . . they are gone . . . to Guerrero."

"Come over here where I can see you!" Tom commanded, still wary that gunmen might be lurking behind the cabin's walls. "When I can see you ain't got a gun,

I'll check inside. I swear I'll kill you, boy, if this is a trick.''

"It is not a trick, señor,'' the boy replied quietly. "They have gone to the cantinas in Guerrero, leaving me to watch the cows, and the stallion.''

"The stallion?'' Tom puzzled over the news that there was a stud horse close by. "What stallion?''

"The big white one. Alla, in the barn.''

Tom swung carefully out of his saddle, covering the front of the cabin with his .44 as the boy walked closer with short, tentative footsteps, keeping his arms raised. Tom could see the boy clearly now, a slender youth, hardly more than half grown.

When Tom was sure the kid did not have a gun, he crept toward the cabin on the balls of his feet, to keep his spurs from rattling over the hardpan. Inching to the door frame, he peered inside with his gun leveled to the room. The cabin was empty. Four rawhide cots lined a wall. A table held the lantern, listing to one side on a broken leg.

Tom turned back to the boy, stepping away from the light behind him to keep him from making an easy target for someone hiding in the darkness. He glanced to the corral again. Two rawboned geldings ate from a pile of loose hay. It started to make more sense that the kid was alone. Four horsemen had herded the cattle to the river, and only two horses stood in the corral, forcing Tom to guess that the other was a spare mount.

"Where's the white stud?'' Tom asked, waving his gun barrel under the boy's chin.

"In the barn, señor. Luis ordered it, that we tie the stallion where no one would see him.''

Tom stepped closer, to place the gun against the boy's ribs. "Who the hell is Luis?"

The boy's eyes rounded when he felt the cold iron. *"El Jefe,* the most famous *pistolero* in all of Mexico!" he gasped. "Surely you know of *El Jefe,* Luis Valdez?"

Tom blinked. Of course he knew the name, but that would be a different Luis Valdez. Too much time had passed for there to be any possibility that it was the same Luis Valdez. Valdez would be an old man now, older than Tom. That Luis Valdez would be too old to ride into Texas to rustle cows. "I knowed a Luis Valdez once," Tom said. "But that was a long time ago. The man I knowed is probably dead. Figures that somebody shot him in the back, most likely, 'cause they couldn't kill him from the front side."

The frightened boy wagged his head side to side. "He is the same man, señor. His hair is white, but his guns are as fast as lightning from the sky! *Verdad!"*

Now it was Tom's turn to shake his head. "Can't be the same one," he stated flatly. "The one I'm talkin' about hasn't been heard from in thirty years. Valdez is a common name down here. It ain't the same Luis Valdez. I'm sure of that."

Though the boy looked doubtful, he repeated himself. "He is the same man, señor. For many years, he has been in prison, but now they release him. The revolution has passed, and he was set free. All the people of Guerrero know him, señor. He is called *El Jefe,* the chief of the *pistoleros."* The boy swallowed. *"El Jefe* has sworn to ride north of the river to rob the *Tejanos* as he did long ago. I am very much afraid of him, and so are the others."

Tom still questioned the news the boy gave him. If he

was adding up the years correctly, he had been riding fences for Captain King back when Luis Valdez terrorized ranches north of the border with his raids.

"Let's have a look at that white stud," Tom said. "I reckon its stolen property, too, like my cows."

The boy seemed relieved when Tom took his gun barrel from its resting place against the boy's ribs. "He is a beautiful stallion, señor," the boy whispered. "Very proud, the way he holds his head up high and prances with his hooves far from the ground."

"Show me," Tom said. "I'll take the stud back with me, to save somebody else the aggravation."

Tom was led to a box stall inside the dark shed. Even in the darkness, Tom could make out the good conformation of a powerfully built white stud. The stallion was tied to a roof beam by a thick sisal rope.

Tom turned to the Mexican youth. "Saddle your horse," he growled. "Then lead that stud out of the stall. You're gonna help me drive that herd of cattle back to the river tonight, and if you do the job right, I won't kill you. When this feller Valdez comes back in the mornin', you can inform him that he damn near made a fatal mistake. Tell him those stolen cattle belonged to T.C. Culpepper, and he goddamn sure better leave my herd alone. You can tell him he was lucky not to be here when I showed up, or he'd be sleepin' in a shallow grave when the sun came up. Make damn sure you tell him what I said, when you get back. Because if he shows up again around Rio Blanco, I'm gonna kill him."

Chapter Four

"I miss the old days," Jessie Kootz said, staring absently at a damp ring on the tabletop left behind by the mug of lukewarm beer he held in his hand. Jessie was toothless and Tom quickly grew tired of listening to Jessie's mushy attempts at clear speech. The old cowboy's lips puckered inward, occupying the space once filled by teeth. It was a reminder that always sent Tom home filled with determination to brush his own teeth vigorously with baking soda, so his mouth would never look like Jessie's.

"I reckon I miss 'em, too," Tom remarked softly, so Consuelo could not hear him. Her comment about his age the day before still rankled him. From the corner of his eye, he could see her pause now and then from her chores behind the bar to listen to their conversation. And he was further angered to learn about Consuelo's influence on Maria Flores, poisoning a young girl's mind with lofty notions about the profession of prostitution. He put Consuelo in a category with cockroaches, eating everything she could while fouling the rest. It was only when urges overpowered him that he was driven to her

41

shack at the rear of the cantina. He always tried to wait until every window in town was dark, hoping no one would notice when he paid her a call. Down deep, he knew everyone in Rio Blanco knew about his visits to Consuelo. It was the nosiest town on earth, Rio Blanco was, and his plight was made worse by living adjacent to Delia Cummings, who was unrivaled in her knowledge of everyone's comings and goings.

Jessie spotted an ant headed across the table with sights set on the sugar bowl. He crushed it with the tip of a calloused finger and then gave a suspicious glance to the empty peach tins at the bottom of each leg of the table. Properly filled with water, the tins provided a moat to drown hungry ants. But in the dry summer heat, the water evaporated quickly, an invitation swarming ants couldn't ignore. "I don't see no future for a cowboy," Jessie said, with a terrible sadness in his voice that spoke for every ranch hand in the vicinity. "Dry as it is, we'll all be out of work when the herds get sold off. Hank took that buyer's offer, Tom. Appears I'll be lookin' fer a new place to hang my saddle before the month is out."

Tom lifted a shot glass of tequila to his mouth, wishing there was something he could offer Jessie, even if it were nothing more than hope. "I can't use a hand myself, Jess," he said, then he tossed back his drink and waited for the burning to subside in his throat. "Sold most of my older cows last year, when it stayed so damn dry. Gave 'em away is what I did. They averaged less than twenty dollars a head by the time I figured my expenses. Maybe Chap's got some day work."

Jessie wagged his head, his expression more sorrowful than ever. "I already asked. Chap said he was near 'bout broke an' can't afford to hire no extra hands. Said

42

if you hadn't got his stolen cattle back, he'd have gone under this fall fer sure.''

Tom poured himself another drink, remembering Chap's refusal to ride over to Mexico to look for his cows. ''Chap has changed,'' he said ruefully. ''He's gone soft. If his pa were still alive, he'd have gone down there with me. Chap wouldn't go. Said he was worried about goin' to jail. Hell, Jess, if a man ain't got the backbone go take back what got stole from him, he ain't . . .'' Tom let his voice trail off before he actually called Chap a coward in front of Jessie. Jessie knew what Tom was trying to say.

Jessie took a noisy swallow of beer, his Adam's apple bouncing up and down inside his slender neck. ''He's just scared, Tom, like everybody else around here. Scared of goin' flat broke, like Hank was set to do without any grass. Chap figures he's next, if it don't hurry up an' rain.'' Now Jessie looked Tom in the eye. ''That was a damn brave thing you done . . . ridin' over all by your lonesome after them rustlers. Nobody'll ever say you're short on nerve. If you'd told me you was goin', I'd have damn sure rode along to lend you a hand. My eyes ain't so good the past few years, but I can still shoot a no-good varmit when I get close enough to see 'em.''

Tom chuckled softly. ''I reckon you already heard that it was Luis Valdez and his gang who stole our cattle.''

Jessie nodded, to say that he already knew. Tom made it a point to tell everyone he ran across this morning. Almost everyone in Rio Blanco had stopped by his corral for a look at the magnificent white stud. It was safe to tell a slightly enhanced version of events down in that Guerrero canyon last night, since he'd been alone. A more exciting depiction of his ride into the robbers' roost

43

wouldn't harm anyone. Folks around Rio Blanco needed a little excitement, to take their minds off the drought.

A noise behind the bar distracted him. Consuelo banged a glass down on top of the bar with enough force to catch their attention.

"Luis Valdez indeed!" she spat, her voice thick with loathing. "If it was Valdez who stole the cows, he is much too old to take them very far. He is old enough to be my grandfather! *Oye!* He is almost too old to walk, if it was the real Luis Valdez of *el revolución!*"

Tom made a face in Consuelo's direction. "What the hell would a *puta gorda* know about a dangerous *pistolero?*" he snapped, suddenly irritated by her intrusion into the conversation, most especially with a remark that took some of the shine off Tom's accomplishment.

Consuelo glared back at him. "I was a little girl when Luis Valdez led his army through Hidalgo," she replied, fleshly jowls aquiver. Her anger did not subside. "You can call me a fat whore if you like, Tom Culpepper, but you can't change the truth! Valdez is an old man now! And so are you, *viejo!*"

Tom was determined to have the last word. "You were never a little girl, Consuelo," he said evenly. "You were always big and fat, even the day you were born."

"Bastardo," she whispered, then she whirled for the shelves at the back of the bar, muttering to herself in rapid Spanish.

Jessie grinned, revealing his empty gums, a sight Tom wished he hadn't seen.

Tom lowered his voice. "She's the reason Arturo ain't got any business these days. Nobody wants to buck-jump a fat woman with a big mouth. Look around at these empty tables."

44

Jessie seemed to contemplating Tom's conclusions, then he shook his head. "It ain't her so much, Tom," he said darkly, as if he were about to share a well-guarded secret. "It's this town that's empty. More'n half the houses are boarded up. Nearly everybody's gone broke around here, because it's so damn dry. I don't figure a fat woman's got much to do with it."

Tom wasn't satisfied, giving Consuelo a sideways glance. "She's a big part of it, Jess. She's runnin' off what little business there is in Rio Blanco. I've about decided to take my business someplace else."

The sounds of a trotting horse distracted Jessie briefly as someone rode to the hitch rail in front of the cantina. "Closest place with a Meskin whore is a day's ride, Tom," he said. "By the time you get to San Ignacio, you're liable to be out of the mood." Then he smiled. "You get to my age, the mood don't strike near as often. Easier to talk myself out of the notion, too."

Boots sounded on the cantina porch. Hank Wardlaw walked in, wiping trail dust from his face with a soiled bandana. He saw Tom and Jessie, the only patrons in the place, and sauntered over to their table. "Howdy, boys," he said, sounding tired. "Mind if I join you?" Without waiting for an answer, he drew back a chair and sat heavily to finish mopping his forehead. "Hot as blazes today," he said, an unnecessary observation among residents of Rio Blanco.

Tom heard the beer keg gurgle behind the counter. Consuelo did not need to ask what Hank wanted to cut the dust from his throat. "I hear you sold out to that cattle buyer from San Antone," Tom said as Hank returned his bandana to his pocket. "Sorry to hear it,

Hank. It won't seem the same around here without cattle carryin' the Wardlaw brand.''

"Got no choice," he replied. "There ain't enough grass out at my place to keep a jackrabbit alive. My cows damn near walked themselves to death lookin' for a blade of grass and a drink of water. My best cows were startin' to look like race horses. Never saw long-horns get so thin. Yours and Chap's ain't all that plump, Tom. You oughta think about sellin', too.''

Consuelo came toward their table carrying a mug of beer with foam sloshing over the rim. "While we're on the subject of plump," Tom began, "have you noticed how fat Consuelo has gotten lately?''

Hank lowered his voice. "She's always been on the plump side, Tom. When a man's sap is on the rise, he ain't inclined to notice such things quite so much.''

Consuelo banged Hank's beer on the tabletop, slop-ping white foam down the sides of the mug. She gave Tom a baleful glare while she waited for Hank to dig a nickel from a pocket of his faded denims, extending a fleshy palm for the coin. Hank handed her a dime. She took her eyes off Tom to look at it, then she turned away without a word and started back toward the bar, her hips swaying.

"She's gotten fatter," Tom said flatly, just loud enough for Consuelo to hear him. "She's the only thing around Rio Blanco that's puttin' on any beef. I was just tellin' Jessie that she's runnin' off Arturo's business. Nobody's gonna pay to buck-jump a woman who's mostly tallow.''

Consuelo looked over her shoulder at Tom. She stuck out her tongue before she disappeared into the little kitchen off the back.

"I heard you rode over the river to get a bunch of stolen cows back," Hank remarked. "Heard they was yours an' Chap's."

Tom took his mind off Consuelo to answer Hank. "I trailed 'em down to those big canyons below Guerrero," he said. "Chap was afraid to go, worryin' about the *Federales*. I wasn't gonna tolerate havin' my cows stole, Hank. Just plain wasn't gonna stand for it. I followed the tracks to a canyon where they were holdin' the herd. Pulled my guns and rode right up to their hideout. I told 'em I'd kill the first son of a bitch who reached for his iron. A bunch of *bandidos* who ride with Luis Valdez took our cattle. They knew I meant business, too. I warned 'em not to come back across that river again or I'd put every last one in a shallow grave. Found a big white stud while I was set to gather the cattle. I figures he was stolen, too. The stud's over at my place now. You oughta drop by and see him before I send word to the Rangers."

Hand was staring at Tom intently. "Luis Valdez. I know that name . . ."

"Muy famoso pistolero," Tom told him. "Got a reputation all over Mexico for being quick on the draw. He just got out of prison, they told me. He's a bad hombre, that Valdez."

"He is a grandfather!" Consuelo shouted from the kitchen doorway. "He is even older than Tom!"

Tom knew she had been listening closely from the kitchen, waiting for the chance to discredit his accomplishment. Anger hardened his cheeks, then he sighed and abandoned the notion to argue with Consuelo about it in front of Hank and Jessie. "He's still a dangerous man," Tom said quietly, addressing the remark to Hank.

"Age don't always slow a man's gun hand. Experience can make some men more deadly."

"You'd know," Hank agreed. "There was a time when nobody along the border had the guts to call you out. Everybody knows you're the reason we never had much trouble in Rio Blanco, back when times were better. Hardcases swung wide of our town when they learned you was our sheriff."

Tom was gratified that Hank remembered. "Now that Luis Valdez knows I run cattle around here, he'll go someplace else to do his devilment. I don't figure we'll have to worry about any more cows disappearin'. I made it real plain what I'd do. Wish Chap had gone over with me, so he'd know just how bad I throwed a scare into 'em. When a man's starin' down a barrel of a gun, he's usually payin' real close attention."

Hank downed the rest of his beer. "It's a damn shame things have to come to an end," he said wistfully, looking out a cantina window at nothing in particular. "Hard times have come to Rio Blanco and it looks like they're here to stay. It ain't never gonna rain, Tom. You'll have to sell out pretty soon, and so will the others. That pool is dryin' up faster than shit runs through a goose. Yesterday, you could see more mud. It's those damn sheep, packin' down the sheep springs. Most worthless animal on earth, a sheep is. Soon as they're born, they're lookin' for a place to lie down an' die. Half the sheep in this county are sick with some sort of affliction every day of their lives. We shoulda passed an ordinance a long time ago, makin' it against the law to own sheep in Rio Blanco."

Jessie nodded his understanding. "I'd just as soon raise a herd of pigs," he said quietly. "Be just as dignified. Pigs are smarter too. A damn *borrego* is about the dumbest creature on earth. Hank's right about what they're doin' to that pool. What springs they ain't packed down with their hooves are covered up with sheep shit.''

Tom knocked back another shot of tequila. "I'd sooner die than own sheep," he agreed. Then he remembered a question he had been wanting to ask Hank. "If it's any of my business, how much did your cows bring?"

Hank's shoulders seemed to drop. "Twelve dollars a head," he said with a sigh. "Burke claimed he was only interested in the hides. He said the meat would be too stringy, damn him."

Tom remembered his dislike for the San Antonio cattle buyer. "I'd rather drown my cattle in the river than take twelve a head for 'em," he said. " 'Specially to that uppity gent in the derby hat. I came within a whisker of puttin' a bullet through him the other day, when he called me an old-timer.''

Jessie grunted and wagged his head. "There ain't enough water 'round here to drown a cow," he said. "If it don't rain pretty soon, all you'll have is piles of cow bones. Twelve a head is better'n nothing. If I owned cattle, I'd sell 'em, same as Hank did.''

A disturbance in the kitchen halted conversation. Arturo limped through the doorway, carrying his wooden bucket and mop, the bald spot across the top of his head shining in the day's glow from the cantina windows. Dreading the lye smell, Tom pushed back his chair and stood up. "I can't stand the stink of lye," he said, when Jessie and Hank gave him a questioning look.

Hank downed the rest of his beer. "I need to be goin' anyway," he sighed, climbing slowly to his feet. "Clara sent me to town to get coffee beans.''

"You wasted a trip," Tom warned, making a turn for the door. "I been without coffee for a week, and the wagon ain't due in from Laredo until next Tuesday."

Hank followed Tom to the door. Jessie's chair scraped back as Tom went out on the cantina porch.

"No coffee," Hank said, sounding disgusted, squinting in the bright sunlight beyond the porch. "Not 'til Tuesday . . ."

"Salvador's only stocking a little stuff now," Tom said, with a glance down the road at the *mercado*. "If he ain't careful, nobody will come to his store for things they need, figurin' he won't have them in the first place."

Hank stood on the shaded porch a moment, wearing a thoughtful expression. "This town's dryin' up, Tom, just like our river. Won't be long until everybody's gone. There won't be any reason to stay."

Tom grimaced, thinking about what Rio Blanco would look like as a ghost town. "Be a damn shame," he said softly, passing a glance over the boarded windows of the mercantile, then the Villareal bakery and café. He tried to count the years since there had been *pan dulce* displayed in the glass case behind the bakery window. He missed those Mexican sweet breads. How long had it been? He couldn't remember. "Swing by and have a look at that stud before you leave town," he added, as Hank stepped off the porch to mount his bay. "Hell of a fine-blooded horse. Pure Spanish Barb, by the look of him."

Hank aimed a look at Tom's house. "I'd better head back," he said. "I've got a windmill to fix before sundown. Damn sucker rod leathers got too dry. Our drinkin' water comes from that well."

"Just like everything else," Tom offered. "I nearly run out of wind before I can pump up any water from my well."

Jessie walked up beside Tom as Hank reined his horse away from the rail. "I'll have a look at that stud," Jessie said, hanging his thumbs in the front pockets of his denims. He looked at Hank. "I'll need to draw my wages pretty soon, boss," he added somewhat sheepishly, as if it embarrassed him to ask.

Hank gave a nod, and again it seemed like his shoulders dropped a little. 'Sorry I had to let you go, Jessie," he said, as though the apology hurt him. "Don't need a cowboy if I ain't got any cows. You ride out tomorrow and I'll scrape together your money."

Hank clamped his spurs into the bay with more force than was necessary. Tom understood. Hank wanted to escape a painful subject as quickly as he could. Jessie had worked for the Wardlaw ranch for more than twenty years.

Tom left the porch, taking only a few steps into the blast furnace heat before a voice from the cantina stopped him.

"Why you no pay for the tequila, Tom?" Consuelo asked, filling the door frame, her fists resting atop the swell of her ample hips.

"I forgot," he replied, which was the honest truth. "Mark down what I owe. I'll pay tonight, after supper."

He swung away from Consuelo, deeply embarrassed by his forgetfulness. It was the damn bucket of lye that caused it, he knew. If Arturo had only waited to begin his relentless mopping. . . .

Chapter Five

"Yessir," Jessie began, "that's some mighty good horseflesh. A blind man can see he's got breeding."

Tom and Jessie rested their elbows on the top rail of Tom's coral to admire the stud. Tom's bay had been confined to the stall in the shed, to allow the stallion to roam the pen where anyone who passed by could see it.

"His owner will be happy to get him back," Tom said. "I asked Jesus Soto to carry a message over to the telegraph office at Encinal tomorrow, so the Rangers will know about the stud."

"He's a damn fine animal, Tom," Jessie continued admiring the horse's long lines, sloping shoulder, and deep heart girth. "I'll bet he can run a hole in the wind."

Tom shook his head. Jessie knew horses. "I aimed to ride him this evening, when it's cooler. Just to see how he gets along under a saddle."

The white stallion stood quietly, its head lowered to be in the scant shade of a withering live oak tree next to the corral fence, its sleek coat mottled in shadows cast by the leaves.

"He'll have an easy gait," Jessie promised. "Long cannon bones. A horse with long cannons always rides like a rockin' chair."

"Luis Valdez learned a lesson from this," Tom said. "By now he knows he better not steal any livestock around Rio Blanco or there'll be hell to pay. Takin' back this white stud will teach Valdez some manners. He knows better than to cross trails with T.C. Culpepper from now on."

"I remember hearin' about Valdez," Jessie said. "Back when I first came to Rio Blanco, he was the terror of the border country. I got to Laredo the day after him an' his gang robbed the bank. Folks claimed Valdez was downright fearless, ridin' up and down the street with both pistols spittin' lead. He used to carry two guns. Did you know that, Tom? Was he wearin' two pistols when you jumped him the other night?"

Tom cleared his throat, wishing for a drink right then. He did not want to tell Jessie an out and out lie, but neither could he tell the absolute truth that would tarnish his story. "It was dark, Jess," he began. "I threw down on the gents in that cabin soon as I rode up. Couldn't exactly see their faces, on account of the dark, or how many sidearms they was wearin' either. I was set to shoot the first hombre to go for a gun. Mostly, I was payin' attention to what they were doin' with their hands."

"Understandable," Jessie replied, still watching the stud. "I reckon I woulda done the same, outnumbered like you was."

Tom swung away from the fence, hoping to leave this subject for another topic. "I've got a bottle of Kentucky corn sqeeze in the house. Let's have a nip or two. Can't stand the smell of that goddamn lye when Arturo starts to mop in the afternoon. And we won't be interrupted by some big-bellied whore if we decide to have ourselves a conversation. Between that fat whore and Arturo's stinkin' mop, all his customers are avoiding the place. He'll go broke in another month or two, 'less he finds a better-lookin' *puta* and puts that mop away.''

Jessie chuckled, showing off his guns. ''If memory serves me right, you used to be kinda sweet on Consuelo,'' he said walking alongside Tom to the back door of his house.

Tom bristled, taking his eyes off the hardpan leading to his back steps to argue the point with Jessie. ''Your memory's gone bad, Jess. I never was sweet on that damn whore!'' Before he could offer further denial, he felt his left boot sink into a pile of chicken droppings below his doorstep, the very thing he'd been trying so hard to avoid with close scrutiny until Jessie made the offending remark. ''Damn,'' he hissed, when he felt the boot move in the slippery substance. He looked below the porch for the spotted dog. ''That goddamn red rooster of Benito's comes over to my yard an' shits all over the place. That worthless dog of mine won't even whimper when it happens. One of these days I'm gonna shoot that chicken an' tie it around the dog's neck until it rots off. If that don't teach him to hate a chicken, I'll shoot the dog and be done with all the worry. Sorriest damn dog I ever owned, Jess. Too lazy to catch his own supper.'' He wiped off his boot sole angrily when he reached the first step.

They entered the cooler interior of the house, Tom hardly noticing the absence of clutter that was proof Rosa had been there today to do his cleaning. He walked to a water-stained cabinet near the stove to remove a bottle of bourbon from its hiding place. "Last one," he said unhappily, straightening to pull the cork. He'd been drinking more lately, which he blamed on stress from the drought. With a pair of glasses from the drainboard where Rosa left them after being washed, he came to the table and poured for himself and Jessie, then he dropped into a cowhide chair.

Jessie raised his glass in a toast. "This is liable to be the last drink you an' me have together," he said, the pupils of his eyes becoming dark pools mirroring his sorrow. "I reckon I'll be pullin' out, soon as Hank pays me my wages. Got to start lookin' for work someplace, I reckon. Sure as hell ain't lookin' forward to ridin' off from this country. Made my home here for quite a spell."

"I'm really sorry, Jess," Tom offered, hoisting his own glass in salute to Jessie's departure. "Wish there was some way I could help. Lots of folks'll miss you around here."

They downed their glasses in silence. Tom tried to think of something else to say, words that might make Jessie feel better. Even darker truths awaited Jessie, Tom knew, when the old cowboy went elsewhere to look for work. Most ranchers would fear the capabilities of a seventy-year-old ranch hand, believing he was too old to do a day's work. And like most ranch hands, Jessie had been unable to save any money from his meager wages. He would be broke, adrift in a world full of younger men competing for cowboying jobs. Tom wondered if Jessie understood how grim his prospects for the future really were.

"I feel sorry for Hank," Jessie said, staring at his

empty glass. "Him'n his boys will wind up bein' hired hands, just like me. That ranch ain't worth a shaker of salt without water. He's busted, only he's too damn proud to admit it. It's a damn shame when a few dry years can wipe a feller out like this." He looked up at Tom. "It's gonna happen to you, Tom, if it don't rain real soon."

A knot began to form in the pit of Tom's stomach. As best he could, he tried not to ever think about the prospects of selling out and moving on. Rio Blanco was home, a place where he felt a sense of belonging. Going someplace else to start over was unthinkable. "I hope it don't," he said quietly, reaching for the bottle to refill their glasses. "I don't know what I'd do if I had to sell . . ."

"Same as everybody else," Jessie remarked, with a note of finality Tom didn't like. "You pack your warbag and move along to greener pastures. If it don't rain, you damn sure can't stay here."

"It'll rain one of these days," Tom countered. "It has to, some time or another."

Jessie gave him a knowing look. "There's the problem for older gents like us. We're runnin' out of time." He ran the tip of his tongue over his sunken lips. "You could say my fuse is lit already. Won't be long 'til yours is, too."

Tom tossed his drink down his throat and quickly poured again. Perhaps the fuzzy softness of the whiskey would loosen the knot in his belly, if he drank enough of it. "I ain't quite as old as you, Jess," he protested. "I've got a little more time for it to rain."

Jessie's expression turned somber. "You may not have as much time as you think," he said quietly, staring off into space. "Not too long ago I thought I had all the time in the world. Woke up one day whilst I was shavin'. Looked in the mirror an' saw an old man, face all wrinkled up like dry shoe leather. Started addin' up the years that mornin'. Scared hell outa me when I discovered I was damn near seventy years old."

Desperately, Tom sought a way to change the subject. It had begun to seem that everyone in Rio Blanco wanted to talk about getting old. "Have you taken a close look at little Maria Flores lately?" he asked.

Jessie's eyes clouded. "You mean Pedro's girl?"

Tom nodded, "She ain't a little girl any longer. She's got bosoms the size of a man's fist underneath her dress. Hardly noticed it 'til the other day, when she brought my laundry. She's gotten as pretty as a speckled pup an' I hadn't paid any attention."

"As big as a man's fist," Jessie sighed. "Young as she is, they won't be all saggy and droopy either."

"Like Consuelo's," Tom remembered, enjoying the unfavorable comparison, wishing Consuelo had been there to hear him make it.

A gust of wind sighed through the live oak trees around the house. Dust swirled across Tom's front yard. A loose window pane rattled in the bedroom, then the wind died and all was quiet. Tom poured Jessie another drink. "Let's drink to young women with firm bosoms," he said, adding a splash of bourbon to his glass.

Jessie didn't appear to be listening, staring out Tom's front windows absently. He brought the glass to his lips and slurped noisily from it. "Got no idea where I'll go," he said thickly. "North, I reckon, maybe up around San Antone. Maybe somebody's gettin' together a trail drive up to Kansas this fall. I know every inch of that Chisholm. I followed herds up there dozens of times."

Tom hated to dash Jessie's idea with hard truth. "The Chisholm's been closed for a number of years, Jess. The last herds went up in '78 or '79. There aren't any more trail drives. They've got railroad spurs nearly every place on earth where there's cows these days."

Jessie looked down at his gnarled hands. Tom couldn't swear to it, but it looked like his eyes were moist. "What's a cowboy to do?" he asked. "Cowboyin' is about all I know . . ."

"You'll find a ranch job someplace," Tom promised, adding inflection to his voice to sound hopeful. "San Antone would be a good place to look."

Jessie tented his thin shoulders and let out a deep sigh. He drained his glass and came slowly to his feet. "I'm obliged fer the whiskey, Tom. I reckon I'd better head out to the ranch to collect my gear. I'll drop by tomorrow, after I draw my wages. That idea of yours about San Antone is startin' to make sense."

They shook hands, Jessie extending his first. Tom took it and pumped his arm once, finding that he was strangely unable to look Jessie squarely in the eye. "Best of luck, pardner," he said, forcing a grin. "You'll be on a ranch payroll before you know it."

Jessie plodded to Tom's front door. He seemed more frail than Tom remembered when he let himself out on the porch. Tom followed him outside, almost blinded by the sun's glare. Jessie clumped down the porch steps, his runover boots dragging when he started down the road as though they weighted down his footsteps.

The spotted dog got up from its resting place below Tom's chair, stretching luxuriously, yawning, as its tail started to wag. Tom saw the movement from the corner of his eye and turned. "Get up, you lazy bastard," he snarled, with as much venom as he could muster to scold his beloved pet. "Get your ass out there and catch a rabbit. It's damn near suppertime and I swear on a stack of Bibles I ain't gonna feed you today, nor tomorrow either. Not one bite of my food goes in your mouth until you catch somethin' of your own. I don't give a damn if you get as thin as a rail this time. Times are hard, in case you hadn't noticed, so get off your lazy ass and chase somethin' to eat, or by God I'll let you starve to death right here on this porch."

The dog came over, passing its tongue over its upper lip in an expectant show of hunger. Then it licked Tom's hand, wagging its tail furiously.

"Won't do any good to beg," Tom warned. "I've made up my mind to teach you a lesson. There'll be one dead dog on T.C. Culpepper's porch unless you start pullin' your share of the load."

The dog whimpered, looking up at Tom with big liquid eyes.

"You act like you hadn't heard a word I said," he complained. Feigning exasperation, he let out a sigh and patted the dog's head. "I swear you're dumber'n a sheep," he added in a gentler voice. "I oughta be downright embarrassed to keep a dog that's too dumb to understand the spoken word. Last dog I had before your worthless ass came along was smarter'n a whip. He could fetch a stick before it hit the ground, an' he kept Benito's goddamn chickens from shittin' all over my yard."

He hadn't seen Delia Cummings until it was too late to hurry inside, intent upon his conversation with the

60

dog. Delia walked along the footpath between Tom's house and Benito Sanchez's adobe with her market basket in the crook of her arm. Her sunbonnet was turned toward Tom's front porch and he knew she had seen him. "Afternoon, Miz Cummings," he said, trying to sound cheerful, though he felt no cheer.

"Good afternoon, Tom," she replied. Then the moment Tom dreaded arrived. She stopped, straightening the front of her dress with a few swipes of her hand. "I see you remembered to wear your pants today, and that awful gun. Some folks feel it isn't necessary for you to wear that gun anymore. These are peaceful times, and that gun only serves as a reminder of bygone days."

A flash of anger went through Tom. "Then I don't suppose you heard that I had to go after a gang of cattle rustlers just yesterday, Miz Cummings," he spat. "Without my guns, me an' Chap Grant would be short by thirty-eight head. If I hadn't been carryin' this gun, about all I coulda done when I found those rustlers is ask 'em real nice if they wanted to give us our cows back. I coulda said please and been real polite about it." He ground his teeth together. "Instead, I stuck this here gun in their faces an' told 'em I'd kill them deader'n fence posts if they ever came back to Rio Blanco. They got pale as ghosts, 'cause they knew I meant to kill 'em. I got our cows back. You may be reminded of bygone days, Miz Cummings, when you see me wearin' this gun, but I damn sure put the fear of God into Luis Valdez and his *pistoleros* with it!"

Delia stiffened. "There's no need to shout, Tom, or to take the Lord's name in vain and use profanity. I simply said that times have changed. You haven't changed with the times, it would seem. When those cows were stolen it was an isolated incident. There hasn't been so much as a hen's egg missing around Rio Blanco for ten years or more that I can remember, not since before my Clarence passed away.''

He was tempted to say that Clarence Cummings surely died from sheer exhaustion, having to listen to Delia night and day until his overworked ears finally ruptured. "That's because I wear this gun," he said instead. "It keeps folks honest. They know I'll use it if I have to, like what happened yesterday."

"That's a doubtful claim," Delia said, lifting her chin slightly after her point was made. "We live among honest citizens. Your gun has nothing to do with it. You've allowed yourself to become something of a relic, Tom, a relic from a more violent time. Those days are gone, thank goodness. Now I must hurry off to the store to buy some coffee beans."

She lifted the hem of her skirt. Basket in hand, she marched off toward the *mercado*. A word from Tom would have saved her many wasted steps through the afternoon heat, if he told her there were no coffee beans at the store. Instead, Tom took great delight in watching Delia parade through piles of chicken droppings around Benito's house on her way to an empty coffee bin at the *mercado*. It would serve her right, he told himself, for calling him a relic.

The unpleasantness of the exchange with Delia reminded him that he needed a drink. He turned to go back inside, almost tripping over the spotted dog seated happily near his heels. "Find a rabbit, you worthless bastard," he growled, stepping around the dog when he regained his balance. "Go hunting or starve. It don't make a damn bit of difference to me."

62

He slammed the door behind him and stalked to the kitchen table, determined to drink enough before sundown to soothe his agitated nerves. Today, it seemed the whole town had turned against him, despite the courage he had shown to go after the cattle rustlers single-handed. All anyone wanted to talk about was how old things were, and how much things had changed. Consuelo Gomez had started all of it when she made that remark about his age, and now the notion was spreading like a prairie fire across Rio Blanco. He had Consuelo to thank for that, planting that awful seed.

He downed a glass of whiskey and poured another, settling back in his most comfortable chair. When it got cooler, he meant to ride the white stud all over Rio Blanco, to serve as a reminder that Tom Culpepper could still handle himself when the chips were down.

Chapter Six

The stud fidgeted when it felt the weight of the saddle, and a slight hump rounded its back when Tom pulled the cinch. "You try to buck me off and I'll work you over with a spur," he promised the horse. Being thrown was the ultimate disgrace for a cowboy. If it happened in front of witnesses, like the small crowd gathered at the cantina, Tom would never hear the end of it. "Consuelo will tell everybody I'm too old to ride a horse," he muttered, watching the stud's ears as he led it away from the fence. "Damn her anyway. She's the one who got all this started."

He cheeked the headstall with his left hand before he lifted his boot to the stirrup. "I swear I'll jerk your head off your neck if you try to pitch," he warned. "At least give me time to swing over the saddle before you pull any dirty stunts."

Gripping the saddlehorn, he swung himself up as quickly as he could, prepared as best he could be for a sunfish jump or worse, if the stud sucked back into a spin. Tom's relief was immediate when the horse merely pranced a few steps forward, arching its graceful neck with its head held high and proud. When he pulled back on the reins the stud responded easily to the command, halting, though still fidgeting underneath him, eager to move. When he let the animal have its head, it struck a soft-gaited trot, lifting its hooves high off the ground. Tom rode toward the cantina, thinking how right Jessie had been about the stud's easy way of traveling.

Dusk had settled over Rio Blanco, cooling the dry brushland. As Tom trotted to the front of the cantina, he counted the saddled horses at the hitch rail. "A good crowd tonight," he said under his breath. He recognized Chap Grant's gelding, and Jesus Soto's pony. He reined the prancing stud to a halt near the cantina door, knowing the sound of hoofbeats would bring everyone outside.

Benito Sanchez came to the doorway first. He smiled, just as Tom was set to make a remark about the chicken droppings in his yard. "A beautiful *caballo,*" Benito said. He looked over his shoulder to call the others in the cantina. *"Amigos!* Come look at Tom's fine horse!" he cried.

Soon others crowded out on the porch . . . Bob and Billy Wardlaw, Jesus Soto, Pedro Flores in his sheepherder's attire, young Joe Spivey and his hired hand, Manuel Delgado. Arturo Benevides left his usual place behind the bar to have a look at the stud. Juan Sandoval was there, too, and Chance Higgins with mud all over his denims that had dried, clinging to his pants legs like plaster, evidence that he'd been down to the pool at the bend in the river to drag some of his older, weaker cows out of the dangerous sucking mud.

"He rides like a dream," Tom said, when he had

everyone's attention. "Handles light as a feather. I hardly have to touch these reins at all."

Jesus Soto was particularly impressed. "He is beautiful, Señor Tom," Jesus declared, his eyes roaming over the stud's glossy coat.

"Wonder who he belongs to." Billy Wardlaw asked. "Somebody's gonna be glad to get him back, Tom."

Other murmured comments reached Tom's ears, but he became distracted suddenly when Consuelo came out on the porch. She wasn't looking at the horse and it annoyed Tom. Her eyes were fixed on him, and there was no friendliness in them. "Do not fall off, Tom," she said, during a moment of silence, folding her arms across her chest just beneath her generous bosoms. "You have no one to take care of you if you fall off and hurt yourself."

Her remark quickly spoiled his enjoyment of the moment. He could not ignore it in front of everyone. His brain slightly awash in the whiskey he'd consumed that afternoon, he decided to put Consuelo in her proper place. "What would a whore know about taking care of an injured man?" he asked, his voice edged with sarcasm.

Consuelo's eyes widened. The ringlets of dark hair framing her face quivered when she shook her head and then spat on the ground below the porch. "I take care of you when you come to my house at night after everyone is asleep!" she snapped angrily. "But no more, Tom! I would rather die!"

She whirled and paraded back through the cantina doorway. A hush had fallen over the group admiring the stud. Then Bob Wardlaw chuckled. "She don't like bein' called a whore, Tom," he said.

The muscles in Tom's cheeks worked furiously. Consuelo had ruined everything. Faces in the crowd were grinning over her remarks and now the stolen horse he recovered was no longer the center of attention. He looked at Arturo. "That woman is a blight on this town, Arturo. Until you get rid of her, I won't set foot inside your place. She ain't fit to work in a decent drinking establishment. She'll run off the rest of your business and then you'll be like Hank . . . he's got a ranch with no cows, and you'll have a cantina with no patrons."

Arturo shrugged helplessly. "I have no one else to help me," he replied quietly. "Something has come between you and Consuelo, Tom. In time, perhaps it will pass."

Tom shook his head side to side. "It'll never pass. I meant what I said, Arturo. I won't come back until she's gone." An idea struck him when his gaze drifted to Pedro Flores. "You could hire Maria to help you. She's near 'bout a grown woman now and pretty as a picture. She could help you sell drinks. Consuelo could still do her whorin' from her shack."

A heavy silence lingered. Pedro looked down at his sandals, as evidence he did not like Tom's idea.

"She's hardly more'n a child," Chance Higgins protested, with a sideways glance at Pedro. "A cantina don't hardly seem a fittin' place for a kid young as Maria."

The stud began to prance impatiently underneath Tom, tugging at the reins to be allowed to move. Tom glanced at the faces on the cantina porch, judging quickly that his suggestion had no one else's approval. "I won't be back," he said, keeping the stud in check until he finished what he wanted to say. He looked at Chap Grant. The rancher owed him a favor for the return of his stolen cows. "If some of the rest of you would back me on this, we'd be rid of that fat *puta* so we could enjoy our drinks in peace and quiet. A man hadn't oughta be forced to listen to insults while he's spendin' his hard-earned money."

"Take it easy, Tom," Chap said, spreading his palms. "You've got a burr under your saddle blanket over Consuelo. Maybe Arturo will talk to her about it. You ain't bein' reasonable. These are mighty hard times for all of us. I'm sure Consuelo needs this job. Where else would she go?"

I'll be damned if I care," Tom growled. "Just so she ain't here." He clamped his heels into the stud's ribs and loosened the reins. The horse lunged away from the hitch rail at a lope, gathering speed as it galloped past the *mercado*. Tom wouldn't look back as he came to the dry river crossing west of town. Just then, he didn't care whether anyone was paying attention to the stud. All that mattered was making his point to the drinkers assembled on Arturo's porch. Until Consuelo Gomez was no longer employed there, Tom Culpepper would not darken Arturo's doorstep again. It was a matter of pride, he told himself, as the stud's strides lengthened beyond the dry riverbed. He let the horse run, carrying him away from Rio Blanco into the purple shadows of evening painting the brushland. No one in Rio Blanco appreciated what he'd done for the town lately. Instead, he'd been forced to endure all manner of unkind remarks . . . complaints from Delia Cummings about his gun and the implication that he was out of date when he wore it. And the remarks by Consuelo about his age, then Jessie's warning that time was running short for him as well. The whole town had turned against him, or so it seemed. No one expressed any gratitude for his daring ride into Mexico to take back what had been stolen from the area.

"I should have left Chap's cattle in that canyon," he told himself as the stud raced over the powder-dry prairie. "He didn't have the guts to go himself. It would have served him right."

He slowed the horse to a trot, then a walk, when he was about a mile from Rio Blanco. When he looked over his shoulder, he caught sight of a faint dust cloud on the horizon south of town. He stopped the stud to study the dust sign. A frown pinched his forehead. Who would be coming toward Rio Blanco so late in the day? The dust rose skyward in a thickening spiral. Whoever it was, they were coming in a hurry and that almost always spelled trouble of some kind.

He reined the stud back toward town. Simple curiosity forced his return. For twenty years, he'd made it a practice to investigate the comings and goings around Rio Blanco, even long after he no longer wore a sheriff's badge. It wasn't official duty that required him to learn the source of the fast-moving dust approaching Rio Blanco. The town was his home and it was his nature to be protective of what little there was left of it.

The horse struck an easy lope. The coming of nightfall blackened the brushlands around Rio Blanco. A few early stars brightened the heavens as Tom rode to the dry riverbed, then down the sloping bank. The horse's hooves clattered over the Rio Blanco's rocky bottom to reach the climb on the opposite side. Darkness prevented Tom from seeing the dust sign now. Judging the distance, whoever was making the dust should be riding into town any moment. He cast a look to the south where the brush met the outskirts of Rio Blanco and found the prairie empty. Galloping abreast of the *mercado,* he glanced toward the cantina and quickly hauled back on the stud's reins. The horse came to a bounding halt. Tom's gaze was fixed on three horsemen, seated on their mounts in front of the hitch rail. Lantern light spilled from the cantina doorway and a pair of front windows across the shadowy shapes of men wearing drooping sombreros. The man in the middle caught Tom's attention. A barrel-chested Mexican with criss-crossed bandoleers hanging from his shoulders stared at Tom when the stud slid to a stop. Pale lantern light was reflected off a pair of pistols tied to the Mexican's waist.

"Valdez," Tom whispered. His right hand moved closer to the butt of his .44.

A hundred yards separated them. Tom held his horse in check and waited. From the corner of his eye, he saw men come out on the cantina porch cautiously, hanging back near the cantina wall. He recognized Chap and one or two more, though he did not take his eyes off the three horsemen to make a better identification of the bystanders.

"You have my horse!" a voice shouted, and now Tom knew the man wearing bandoleers was Luis Valdez.

The silence that followed was eerie, lingering. Tom's throat had gone dry. Every muscle in his body tensed. "He's mine now," Tom replied hoarsely, as if something were stuck in his throat. "I figure he belongs to somebody else. We'll let the Texas Rangers decide. You stole our cattle. I told the boy to warn you . . . that I'd kill you if you tried it again."

The Mexican gave a dry laugh. He turned to his companions on either flank. *"Tejano estúpido,"* he snapped, then he looked back to Tom. "You are a fool!" he cried.

71

His right hand inched closer to a pistol. "I give you one chance, *Tejano!* Give me back my horse, or I, Luis Valdez, will claim your life!"

No one stirred on the cantina porch. The silence grew heavy, ominous. At a hundred yards, Tom knew it would take a lucky shot for either man to down the other. And there were two of Valdez's *pistoleros* who had to be taken out of the fight. Tom didn't like the odds.

"May not be quite that easy," he said, keeping his voice low. "I've got friends in that cantina. Could be you've forgotten how to count."

Valdez laughed again. Tom saw the gleam of his teeth in the light from a window.

"Your friends have no guns," he said, still grinning. "It is you who must learn how to count."

The stud took a prancing step sideways. Tom tightened the reins even more without taking his eyes from the Mexican's gun hand. "I'm faster," Tom said evenly. "You've got my word . . . you'll be the first to die."

The Mexican's grin faded. His lathered brown gelding stamped impatiently at a fly. It was the distraction Valdez had been waiting for. His right hand clawed for his gun.

Tom's arm was in motion at almost the same instant, his fingers curling around the pistol grips, trigger finger snaking through the loop of the trigger guard as his thumb sought the hammer of the .44. His arm jerked upward in a single, fluid movement. He cocked and aimed simultaneously, then he squeezed the trigger and felt the Colt explode in his fist.

Twin concussions echoed off the front of the cantina and Rogers Blacksmith Shop across the street. Tom heard the whine of a bullet pass his ear and felt its hot breath across his cheek. The white stud bolted when the gun went off near its ears, swinging Tom out of the saddle seat until he caught himself with his free hand. The Mexicans' horses shied away from the dual explosions. Tom cursed his aim silently, knowing he had missed Valdez by mere inches in the half dark.

Another gunshot roared before Tom could settle the stud. Sizzling lead whispered though the air above his head. He swept his gun barrel across the shapes of moving men and horses, seeking Valdez. People were diving off the cantina porch, running in all directions, briefly drawing his attention from his target. Suddenly a horse came charging toward him, a dark blur against the pale background of the caliche road. Tom dug his heals into the stud's ribs to meet the headlong charge. His aim jostled by the powerful lunges of the horse to reach full stride, he thumbed back the hammer of his Colt and waited for a shot that could not miss as the galloping horses came closer together.

The outline of the Mexican's sombrero filled his sights. He dropped the muzzle slightly and nudged the cold iron trigger. A blast thundered from the mouth of his Colt and he felt the shock all the way to his shoulder. A finger of yellow flame stabbed through the darkness. Then he heard the sickening whine of a spent slug above the rumble of pounding hooves and he knew his shot had missed.

He heard a gun crack and saw a muzzle flash. Something slammed into his ribs with the force of a mule's kick. Despite his attempt to stay in the saddle, he was torn sideways, his empty hand clawing feebly for his saddlehorn. Now things happened with syrupy slowness, as though in a dream. He felt himself falling, tumbling helplessly toward the ground. A white-hot pain shot through his left side, then he landed hard on his back, skidding along the caliche hardpan with his arms and legs windmilling, beyond his conscious control. He heard himself grunt when his fall drove the air from his lungs. Suddenly, he couldn't breathe. Stunned, he could only look up at the stars in the night sky overhead, powerless to move when his limbs collapsed on the road. Pain spread quickly across his chest and he wondered if he might be dying.

With all his might, he tried to close his right hand around the butt of his gun, for now he heard the approaching hoofbeats clearly. His fingers curled and met his empty palm . . . he had dropped his gun during the fall.

An involuntary groan escaped his throat just as the rumble of hooves ended close by. He'll kill me now for sure, Tom thought. He was defenseless, and too weak to even raise his head to see the face of the man who had bested him in a duel.

A kaleidoscope of tangled thoughts raced through his mind all at once. Long ago, back when he made his living with a gun, he had wondered what it would be like to die from a gunshot. The men he killed gave him no hint of what lay in store for a bullet's victim. All of them had died without uttering a word as Tom stood over them, savoring his victory. Now a turn of the dice handed him the experience he wondered about. The waves of pain, so close to the spot where his heartbeat was the strongest, promised a speedy end to things. He knew he had just one regret over the lives he had taken with a gun. That boy's face had haunted Tom for years. All the others had deserved to die, for like himself, they laid claim to the gunslinger's profession. There was only the boy who called him out at Carrizo Springs that day to darken his list of accomplishments. If only he had turned his back on the kid's challenge and walked away from it. Pride had gotten in the way.

Spurs clanked over to him and stopped. Tom looked up through eyelids slitted with pain, to see the face of the man standing over him. In the shadow of a broad-brimmed sombrero, he tried to make out the man's features. Slowly, his eyes focused on the grinning countenance of Luis Valdez.

"Estoy mas rapido," Valdez said hoarsely. "I was faster," he added in thickly accented English. "Now I take back my horse, and some of your cows, *Tejano.* Your amigos will not help you. They are nothing but cowards!"

Tom tried to think of something to say, words that might rob Valdez of a part of his victory. But his mind was a blank, for now the pain in his chest grew much worse and he was sure he was losing consciousness by slow degrees. Strange thoughts kept swimming into his mind as he lay dying . . . the boy whose life was ended by Tom's bullet that day in Carrizo Springs, and how deeply that killing had affected him thereafter. Something inside Tom had changed after that and he'd given up the shootist's profession to live quietly in Rio Blanco raising cattle and sheriffing. But why was he thinking about it now?

Soft footsteps running toward him took his attention from Valdez and the painful memories at Carrizo Springs. Someone stepped between him and Valdez, a figure he did not recognize in the darkness.

75

"Vamos!" a woman's voice cried. *"Dejelo morir en paz."*

There was something about the voice that was familiar, yet as the pain dulled his senses, he couldn't be sure. He felt himself slipping toward a swirling gray fog. He tried to remember what the woman had said. "Let him die in peace," and then he understood that he was truly dying.

One last sound reached his ears. The woman spat loudly, then she cried, *"Andale, viejo!"* At last, he knew the woman's identity. His final conscious thought was astonishment. Why was Consuelo showing him any kindness?

Chapter Seven

Hazy images came and went. Time had no meaning. Blurred faces would appear suddenly in the fog around him, then disappear. Now and then he heard voices, but the words were indistinguishable, nonsense. He was aware of the sensation of pain, though he never knew its source; it was simply there. It was as if he were floating a few feet above the ground, twisted slowly about by an invisible sea. When he could focus his thoughts, he wondered if this dark void where he found himself was some sort of entryway into hell. He knew little about such matters, only a smattering of scripture. There was said to be a hell and a heaven and he'd known all along that his misdeeds would sentence him to damnation. Wherever he was now, however, there were no fires to roast him for eternity. In fact, he was cold most of the time.

A face took shape before him, a fuzzy, unrecognizable face that seemed to dance before his eyes. A voice spoke to him in jibberish, meaningless sounds. He tried to answer with a question, asking where he was. But his voice made no sound at all, though he tried to speak with all his might until the face dissolved into blackness. Again, he was alone.

Gradually, he grew more aware of the pain. A dull ache he noticed before became an angry throbbing in his left side. He attempted to reach for the source of it and found that he couldn't move his hands. It was as though he had no body, only a head and the desperate thoughts trapped inside it.

Some time later, he felt something on his tongue and he swallowed it. The sensation came again and he repeated the swallowing, but when he tried to see who had put the liquid in his mouth, he saw only more inky darkness. He could have been at the bottom of a cave, like the caverns he explored near his boyhood home on the Middle Brazos. It was dark in those caves, and chilly, even in summer. Was he in a cave now? Or was this some roadway into hell?

"Tom? Tom?" He recognized his name when the voice spoke to him.

"Where . . . am . . . I?" he croaked, and this time he heard himself speak. His eyelids fluttered open and he saw light, a light that hurt his eyes. He tried to get his bearings. Where was he?

Wooden rafters above his head came into focus first, then walls of rough planking. He was in a room and the room looked vaguely familiar. At least he wasn't in hell, or that dark cavern anymore.

"You are home," a woman's voice said gently. A cool rag was passed over his forehead by the woman who spoke. When he saw her face, he was puzzled. He knew her, and he wondered why she was there.

"What happened?" he asked in a scratchy voice. "I remember being shot. I fell . . ."

Consuelo bent over him. Tiny beads of perspiration clung to her forehead, a brow knitted with concern. "Your wound is very bad, Tom," she said softly. "You have fever, and there is much swelling where the bullet went through."

As if by command, renewed waves of pain gripped his left side and in spite of himself, he groaned. "Why . . . are you here?" he asked, gritting his teeth until the pain subsided.

The frown on Consuelo's face disappeared. "There is no one else to care for you," she whispered. "Chance offered to take you to Laredo in his wagon to see a doctor, but others feared that the drive would kill you in your weakened condition. Someone was needed to care for you until you are stronger . . ."

"Miz Cummings," he interjected before she was finished. "Delia would have looked after me, maybe. I reckon she would, seein' we're neighbors."

Consuelo shook her head. "There is only me, Tom," she sighed, cooling his face again with the damp rag. "No one else offered to help you. Chance made the offer of his wagon. Jessie and some of the others have been by to see you, but you were asleep. Your fever was very bad at first. *Dios!* Your skin was on fire."

Another question popped into his head. "How long have I been asleep?"

Consuelo looked up at the roof, counting the days. "A week yesterday. The first two days, you almost stopped breathing, and you lost so much blood I was certain you would die. I offer prayers to the Blessed Virgin . . . there was nothing else anyone could do."

His mind had begun to clear, and with it came recollections of the gunfight with Valdez. "I'm obliged for what you've done, Consuelo," he said, reading her face. "I can't figure why you'd offer to help me. You and me ain't exactly been on the best of terms lately."

She dipped the cloth in a pan of water on the night stand and dabbed it over his cheeks. "You hurt my feelings, when you said I was too fat. You made me angry, Tom. I wanted to hurt you, so you would know how I feel."

Right then, he wanted to change the subject. Talking about such personal things started to make him uncomfortable. "I reckon Valdez took the white horse," he said quietly.

Consuelo nodded. "And your saddle and bridle," she added. "Some cows are missing, too. Chap sent Jesus and Encinal to send a wire to the Texas Rangers. The Rangers are expected very soon."

"Won't do any good," he sighed, slowly lifting his right hand to touch the strip of cloth covering his wound. He winced and took his hand away. "Valdez is safe in Mexico. Rangers won't be able to do a damn thing."

"*Verdad,*" she said in agreement. "There is nothing anyone can do now."

Despite his weakened condition, he grew angry. "Like hell! Soon as I'm well enough to sit a horse I'll go back down there and square things with Valdez. My aim was bad the other night. Next time we meet I won't be tryin' to stay astraddle my horse. That stud made me miss, but it damn sure won't happen again."

Consuelo placed the rag over his forehead. "Perhaps it was not the stud," she said thoughtfully, as worry returned to her face.

"That's all it was," he replied angrily. "I had Valdez in my sights until the stud threw my aim off. And I was faster, too. He went for his gun first, but I beat him to the draw."

She looked down at him, chewing her bottom lip, as though she had something important to say. "Perhaps your eyes are not as good as they used to be, Tom."

Anger stiffened his limbs. "You're sayin' I'm too old?" he snapped, daring her to answer the question. "There ain't a goddamn thing wrong with my eyes, woman!"

She stood up from the chair beside his bed, still gazing down at him. "You fired your *pistola* twice, and both times, you miss," she remembered aloud.

"It was on account of that damn horse!" he cried, lifting his head from the pillow until the movement caused a knife-edged pain around his wound. He fell back on the bed and groaned. "I already told you it was the horse," he added, tight-voiced. A cold sweat popped out on his skin and now his stomach was churning. He groaned again, more softly this time. "Damn that hurts," he whispered.

"I have some chicken broth on the stove," she said, making a half turn for the bedroom door. "It will help you get your strength back. I will start a fire. Rest now, if you can."

She left him while he was still boiling mad over the remark she made about his eyes. "There ain't a goddamn thing wrong with my eyeballs,' he muttered. "What the hell does a *puta gorda* know about eyes in the first place? She acts like I'm nearly blind."

He would never had admitted it, of course, but lately it had become harder to read the San Antonio newspapers that came with the freight wagon from Laredo. Quite by accident he had discovered that it helped to hold the pages at arm's length. Then the letters weren't quite so fuzzy. But at a distance, he was sure he could see like an eagle. Besides, he would look ridiculous wearing spectacles when he went down to challenge Valdez to a gunfight. "What the hell does she know?" he added softly. "She can claim to be an expert on gettin' poked, but she don't know a damn thing about eyeballs."

His anger cooled as he remembered the duel with Valdez. The Mexican got off a lucky shot, while Tom's aim was ruined by the gait of a galloping horse. He recalled having Valdez in his gun sights when he pulled the trigger on his second shot. "It was that damn stud that done it," he grumbled.

Later, a delicious smell wafted into the bedroom on the breath of a gentle breeze from the kitchen windows. His stomach gave a low growl. It was good to feel hungry, good to feel anything besides the pain in his side. Thinking about the soup, he puzzled over Consuelo's presence at the house. He would have bet his last dime that she hated him, after their exchanges the other day. They had traded insults a number of times. Why had she offered to care for him? It didn't make any sense.

He heard her sandals padding toward the bedroom. She came through the door balancing a bowl of broth on her palm. She smiled when she found him watching her. "I put some juice from the peyote root in it to help with the pain," she said, coming over to the edge of the bed.

"Peyote root?' he asked. "What the hell is that?"

She settled down beside him and lifted a spoonful of

hot soup to his lips. "The medicine plant of *los Indios,*" she told him, tipping the soup into his mouth. "It makes you dream strange dreams. It drives evil spirits from your body. I walked down the riverbank to look for one the day they brought you to your house. I cooked the pulp and placed it over your wound. Some of the juice is in the broth. My mother learned the *curandero's* secrets when she was a girl."

The soup was delicious, salty. "Thanks," he said between spoonfuls. "Still can't figure why you'd do this for me."

A slow smile crossed her face. "I have forgiven you for the bad things you said to me, Tom. We can still be friends."

He scowled. "You started it," he protested. "You started it when you said maybe I was gettin' too old to need a woman."

She forced more soup into his mouth. "You stopped coming to see me at night. When you came to the cantina, you did not look at me. I only wanted you to notice me. I was lonely."

His scowl only deepened. "Whores don't get lonesome," he said as though it was fact. "All you wanted was my money."

Her expression darkened. "I need money, like everyone in Rio Blanco. When you were sheriff, you took the money people paid you to keep the law."

"There's a difference," he insisted quickly. "Sheriffin' is a job. Bein' a whore is gettin' paid to have fun. It ain't the same. A sheriff has got to have principles, which a whore ain't got."

Consuelo halted the spoon midway to Tom's mouth, spilling a little on the front of his nightshirt. Her black eyes began to smolder. "Do you think I have fun when a stinking cowboy comes to my house who does not wash himself for a week? Sometimes, I send them away. It is not true when you say I have no principles."

"It ain't quite the same thing," Tom went on, exasperated by her refusal to admit there was a difference. He attempted to lift his head again and was rewarded by a fresh wave of pain. He groaned and lay back on the pillow. "Bein' a whore is about the lowest profession on earth," he added in a tired voice. "It goes against the scripture."

She banged the spoon into the bowl of soup and bolted to her feet beside the bed. Her eyes were alight with fire. *"Bastardo!"* she hissed between clenched teeth, then she raised the bowl shoulder-high and promptly dropped it to the floor with a crash.

"Why the hell'd you do that?" he asked, so startled that he blinked. "All I said was that whorin' went against scripture . . ."

Consuelo placed her hands on her hips. "Find a holy woman to make your soup!" she cried, the flesh beneath her chin quivering with rage. "Look for a woman who will read to you from the Bible. I am going back to the cantina!"

She wheeled about and marched through the bedroom door. When she left the house, she almost slammed the front door off its hinges. He listened to her footfalls until the sound faded, then he let out a sigh. "It ain't the same as bein' sheriff," he muttered. "Nobody in his right mind can say that whorin' is like keepin' the peace."

He stared at the ceiling for a time, until he started to notice a strange fuzzy sensation in his arms and legs.

84

And his thoughts would not focus, his mind drifting to odd, colorful scenes that made no sense. "What the hell did she put in that soup?" he wondered aloud. "She called it . . . peyote."

As a curious aside, the pain from his wound lessened. When he touched his bandage with a rubbery finger he could barely control, he felt no pain at all. "Powerful stuff," he mumbled, his lips numb like he'd been out in the cold.

Moments later, he closed his eyes, noticing that his sense of balance was gone. Things tilted at odd angles. Bright colors flashed before his eyes, then vanished altogether. An uneasy feeling awoke in his brain. Something had taken control of his thoughts. Though his pain was gone, he didn't like what was happening. It was akin to being on a runaway horse without a pair of reins.

He awakened sometime during the night to strange sounds. Someone was in the room, but he couldn't clear his head well enough to ask who it might be. He heard water pouring and then the damp rag was slapped roughly across his forehead, as if someone meant to throw it for reasons he couldn't explain.

"Who's there?" he was finally able to ask. The room was dark as pitch.

"A sister of the Order of Mary Magdalene," a woman replied in a gritty voice. "Go back to sleep. I will pray for your lost soul."

His sleep-fogged mind couldn't quite grasp what was said. There were no Catholic sisters in Rio Blanco, he was sure. "That'll be a comfort," he mumbled sleepily. "I prob'ly need all the help I can get."

Seconds later, he was fast asleep. There were no more of the odd dreams now. Instead, he found himself in the middle of a street he remembered. Fifty yards away, a kid with a gunbelt tied around his waist was leering at him. Suddenly, Tom knew where he was. He was standing in front of the Broken Spoke Saloon in Carrizo Springs. The slender boy had challenged him to a test of the draw, and when Tom saw his face closely, he knew the boy was about to die.

"Go for your gun," the kid said, full of the courage of youth and inexperience. A crowd watched the proceedings from the boardwalk in front of the saloon.

"I never pull on another man first," Tom heard himself say, the same words he'd spoken to the boy a long time ago. "If you think you're faster, then fill your fist with iron. I don't want to kill you, son, but I damn sure will if you touch that gun."

The kid's leer only widened. He was sure of himself. "I'll put a slug through you before you can clear leather, old man," he said, with an arrogance untested against men in the gunslinger's trade.

"Suit yourself." Tom's reply echoed from the darkest recesses of his memory. "Pull, whenever you think you're ready."

Just once, in the fractions of a second before the boy's hand dipped toward his holster, Tom saw a flicker of doubt in his eyes. But the doubt was gone when eighteen-year-old Billy Clay reached for his pistol. Tom hadn't known the boy's name until it was carved into the wooden plank marking his grave by the Carrizo Spring's undertaker.

The kid's draw was awkward, painfully slow, and only then did Tom realize how badly overmatched Billy Clay was against him. Tom drew smoothly and fired as a reflex, before the kid's fingers could curl around the butt of his gun. There was plenty of time to look at the boy's face when Tom's .44 slug passed through him. Shock and surprise brought a bulge to Billy Clay's eyes as he was lifted off his feet by the force of impact at close range. Tom watched the boy collapse on his back in the wagon ruts in front of the saloon, blood pumping from a hole in his chest. His feet twitched with death throes, then he groaned and went still.

A queasy sickness knotted Tom's belly. He turned away from the fallen kid, his throat filled with bitter bile. There was no satisfaction over the contest. In his heart, he knew he had killed a mere boy who never stood a chance against him. He could easily have ignored the challenge and walked away. His reputation as a shootist was well known along the Rio Grande. He could only blame his pride for the senseless killing he performed at Carrizo Springs.

As he walked away from the lifeless form sprawled in the middle of the road that day, a little voice inside his head told him that this killing would be his last. It was time to do something else with the years he had left. His days as a gunslinger were over.

Chapter Eight

Ranger Captain Bob Hardin introduced himself and Deputy Dick Cole. Hardin was in his forties, Tom guessed, a hard-twisted man, rawboned, with big hands and piercing blue eyes. A handlebar mustache adorned his angular face, flecked with streaks of gray. Tom judged the ranger was every bit as tough as he looked. Cole was much younger, still a greenhorn by Tom's standard, but with a certain hardness about him that held promise. The pair stood beside Tom's bed. When Rosa let them into the house, she'd seemed worried by their arrival and she left quickly after showing them to the bedroom.

"We came as soon as we could," Hardin said. His voice was a slow monotone, betraying no emotion. "The post at Laredo is undermanned, so we couldn't spare anyone for a few days. Sorry."

Tom merely nodded, propped up on two feather pillows in his nightshirt, thinking how foolish he looked.

"Tell us what happened," Hardin continued, hooking his thumbs in his gunbelt. A heavy Walker Colt .44 rested against his right hip.

"Feller by the name of Luis Valdez rode over and stole thirty-eight head of cattle," Tom began, sorting through events to get them in proper order. "I followed the tracks to the border, then I went across to get our cows back. Trailed 'em to a canyon south of Guerrero and that's where I found the herd. I stuck a gun in a Mexican's face who was guarding the cattle and told him I'd come after my livestock. There was a big white Spanish stud horse there, too. I knew damn well he was stolen, same as the cows, so I brought him back. A couple of days later, those *bandidos* came to Rio Blanco. Three of 'em, and I had to face 'em alone. Their leader is Luis Valdez, Cap'n Hardin. You may remember him . . . remember the name. A few years back he was a big name *pistolero* along the border. When I was sheriff of Rio Blanco we had wanted circulars on him all the time."

The captain nodded. "I've heard of him. It was a while back . . ."

Tom hastened to continue with his story, before Hardin started counting the years. "He went for his gun an' I drew down on him. I was ridin' the big white stud. Damn horse shied and threw my aim off. That's when I caught this slug. Don't remember much after that. He took the horse and a dozen cows this time. The cattle will be in that canyon below Guerrero. Horse, too, I reckon."

Hardin took a deep breath, glancing at his deputy. "About all we can do is fill out a report on it, Mr. Culpepper. The river stops us cold, but then I figure you know that already, since you said you used to wear a badge."

"It ain't gonna stop me," Tom said, "soon as I get healed up so I can ride."

"You'll be breakin' the law," Hardin explained needlessly.

Tom simply shrugged, feeling his temper go on the rise.

"They can toss you in jail down there," Hardin added. "They can keep you there long as they want. You'd be better to file a formal request with the *comandante Federal* in Guerrero."

"I'd be dead of old age before anything was done about it," Tom replied. "My way's better."

The captain almost smiled. "You didn't fare so well the last time you tangled with that bunch. From what that woman told me down at the cantina, you damn near died from that gunshot wound."

Tom bristled. "That woman down at the cantina has got a big mouth and an empty head. God gave a turkey more sense than He gave her. Valdez got off a lucky shot while I was tryin' to control that damn horse. Next time, I'll be ready for him."

Hardin's expression turned serous. "There's things you oughta consider, like the fact that you ain't as young as you used to be when you made a name for yourself. Age slows a man down, if you ain't figured that by now. Fact is, Valdez is gettin' on in years himself. It'd be smarter to let the law handle it. Otherwise, somebody's liable to get killed over a few head of cattle. Seems a waste."

Tom couldn't control his anger any longer. Someone else was saying that he was too old to get a job done. Trembling with a mixture of weakness and rage, he pushed himself up on one elbow and fixed the captain with a hard look. "I may not be as young as you figure I need to be, Cap'n Hardin, but that's just one man's opinion. I can still shoot straight, when I ain't aboard some addle-brained horse, an' I can damn sure handle the likes of Luis Valdez. I'd sooner take up knitting than file an official complaint with the *Federales*. Valdez stole my cows and I damn sure aim to get 'em back. If I have to kill him, it comes with the territory. When a man steals somethin' from me, he'd better be ready to pay for it in blood."

Deputy Cole spoke before the captain could replay. "Old codger like you has got no business carryin' a gun. It'll get you killed, mister."

Now Tom directed his anger at the deputy. "I may look like some old silver-haired codger to you, sonny, but my gun hand is as quick as it ever was. If I wasn't laid up here in this bed, I'd prove it to you. Just 'cause my hair is gray and I'm dressed up like a damn fool in this nightshirt, it don't mean I can't put some gent on Boot Hill!"

"Take it easy, Mr. Culpepper," Hardin protested, spreading his palms. "No call to get so riled up about what my deputy said." He dropped his hands and turned for the doorway. "Officially, there's nothing we can do, but I promise you I'll look into the matter and have a talk with the *comandante* over in Guerrero. Maybe that'll throw a scare into Luis Valdez, when he knows the Texas Rangers are on the lookout for him."

Tom settled back against the pillows. His wound was throbbing now. "Tell the *comandante* you've got a message for Valdez from T.C. Culpepper," he growled, placing a hand over the bandage around his ribs, hoping to lessen the pain. "Tell him Valdez is a marked man, as soon as I can get out of this damn bed. Tell him I'm comin' for him, to settle the score. Luis Valdez is a dead man. You can tell that to the *comandante!*''

By the look on the captain's face, he was amused. "I reckon I'll let you deliver that message on your own," he said starting for the door, spur rowels rattling over the floor. "I'll give you a piece of advice, Mr. Culpepper. Stay on this side of the Rio Grande and let the law take care of this. You're really quite a famous feller, T.C., and it'd be a damn shame if you got yourself killed over a few head of thin-hided longhorns." He glanced out Tom's bedroom window. "This is the driest country I ever saw," he added, on his way out of the room. "Don't look like it's rained in a coon's age . . ."

The Rangers shuffled out the door. Tom could see their horses tied to his front porch rail. A gentle southerly breeze blew through the window, allowing him to hear the Rangers' remarks as they mounted.

"That ol' coot is a windy son of a bitch," Deputy Cole said, swinging a leg over his saddle. "He's too damn old to go chasin' all over northern Mexico with a gun. Somebody'll kill him deader'n pig shit if he tries it. I suppose it's downright laughable, a couple of old codgers goin' at each other with a pistol. You said Luis Valdez had to be gettin' close to sixty . . .''

Captain Hardin swung his horse away from the porch. Tom was so boiling mad that he almost forgot to listen to the rest of what was said. Hardin leaned out of his saddle to hawk up a ball of phlegm before he spoke. "There was a time when T.C. Culpepper was considered one of the fastest guns around, Dick. I was a rookie Ranger when he gunned down Bill Allison in front of the Saint Anthony Hotel up in San Antone. It was self-defense, so Culpepper never went to jail for it. The truth is, most everybody was glad to see Allison fitted for a pine box. I remember hearin' about it right after it happened. That had to more'n twenty-five years ago.''

Both Rangers started their horses in motion away from Tom's house, but it did not prevent Tom from hearing the rest of what was said before they rode out of earshot.

"Maybe he was that good with a gun twenty-five years ago," Cole remarked. "But hell, Cap'n, I wasn't even born back then. He'll be slower'n a jug of molasses in wintertime by now."

"Maybe," Hardin replied, his voice becoming distant, hard to hear. "Time changes some things, that's fer sure. Still, I can think of lots of things I'd rather do than go against T.C. Culpepper with a gun. He could still be fast enough to send a feller to an early grave."

Tom's head sank into the pillows. A grin wrinkled his face for a time. "It was downright decent of that Ranger to say what he did," he muttered to himself. "Maybe he's a better gent than I figured he was . . ."

A sound drew Tom's attention to the bedroom door. The spotted dog peered around the door frame, licking its lips, whimpering a greeting to its master, tail wagging.

"How the hell'd you get in?" Tom asked gruffly, the tone he always used when he spoke to the dog. "I reckon those lawmen let you sneak by 'em when they went out." His eyes roamed down the dog's ribs to its flank. "You're gettin' as fat as Consuelo, you no-good bastard," he added, maintaining the stern quality of his voice. "I know damn good an' well you ain't caught a rabbit lately. Somebody's been feedin' you my vittles, damn your worthless hide. I suppose you can stay in the house for a spell, 'til somebody comes along to let you out. But if you shit on my floor, I'll make you sleep in it tonight, so be mighty damn careful while you're here.''

The dog trotted over to the bed, its claws pattering lightly over the floorboards, to place its head on the edge of the mattress near Tom's hand.

Tom patted the dog gently, which brought forth another whimper and more tail-wagging, while big liquid eyes watched his face. ''Stop the goddamn begging,'' Tom complained, stroking the dog's fur with his fingers. ''You're already so fat you can hardly squeeze through my front door. You'll be bigger'n that fat whore before you know it. Fat dogs are near 'bout as useless as fat women. I'm through payin' the feed bill for both of you.''

He thought about Consuelo briefly. This morning, he remembered her visit during the night, when she slapped the wet rag over his forehead, claiming to be a Catholic sister in the dark. ''Women!'' he spat, rubbing the dog's neck affectionately. ''I hope the bitch don't ever come back!''

He swallowed the spoonful of warm broth with his eyes closed. He wouldn't look at Consuelo or say a word to her, not if he could help it. She had come to his house just before sundown, to begin banging pots and pans in his kitchen, creating such a racket that he could not sleep. That afternoon, he had somehow struggled to the edge of the bed to use the chamberpot. In the heat, the smell of urine was stifling and he regretted relieving himself.

''If you're hell-bent to bang pots around this house,

you can toss out that chamberpot under the bed,'' he said, without opening his eyes. ''Stinks worse'n Arturo's mop bucket. I'll figure a way to do it myself if you refuse.''

She dropped the spoon into the bowl and got up with a sigh. ''I should pour it over your head,'' she said quietly, bending down to pick up the pot. ''It would serve you right, for the things you said to me yesterday.''

''I was only tellin' you the plain truth,'' he answered back. ''I was quotin' scripture. Not a damn thing wrong with that.''

She stood above him at the edge of the bed, holding the chamberpot aloft. ''Hold your tongue, Tom Culpepper,'' she warned, moving the pot to a position over his body . . . he saw it through the slits of his eyelids. ''I will visit a priest if I wish to hear a quote from the Bible. You are not a priest, so be silent.''

He waited until she was almost out of the room. ''I'll wager I know a damn sight more scripture than you!'' he spat. Then he turned his face to a window, trying to push Consuelo from his mind. A red sunset colored the western sky. Not a cloud was visible anywhere and he gave up the notion of thinking about rain. He heard Consuelo toss the contents of the pot off his back porch. ''Maybe I'll have some luck and she'll drown that goddamn rooster of Benito's,'' he whispered.

Off in the distance, Pedro Flores's donkey brayed. ''Wish he'd feed that jackass so I could get some rest,'' he muttered. It was as if nothing was going to suit him now. Being confined to his bed only made matters worse. But the pain below his rib cage still went through him like a red-hot poker when he moved too quickly or tried to sit on the edge of the mattress. Until the swelling went down, there was little else he could manage besides bed rest.

Consuelo returned with the empty pot, then she resumed feeding him the soup. He ate with his eyes open now, but wouldn't look her squarely in the face. When the last drop of soup was consumed, Consuelo got up and went to the kitchen. Not a word was said between them during the meal.

Moments later, Consuelo returned with Tom's straight razor and the mug of shaving soap. She placed them on the nightstand beside his bed and picked up the wash basin.

"What the hell are you aimin' to do?" he asked.

For an answer, she took down the shard of mirror hanging above the basin and showed him his reflection. Matted tangles of red and gray curls hung down to his shoulders. More than a week's worth of gray beard stubble covered his cheeks and chin. "I will shave you," she said, starting out of the bedroom with the pan.

"I ain't lettin' you near my throat with a razor," he warned. "Fetch me a pan of water and I'll do it myself, so I'll know my head will still be fastened to my neck when I'm done."

She ignored the remark and went outside. In the evening quiet, he soon heard the sounds of the pump jack from the back of the house. While she was out of the room, he reached for the mirror and took another look at himself.

"Damn," he whispered. "I look worse'n that spotted dog."

The pumping sounds lasted much too long, then they stopped. He waited, growing more impatient by the minute, wondering what was keeping her. A full ten minutes later, the back door banged shut.

"I had to borrow water from Mrs. Cummings," Consuelo said, coming to the nightstand with a pan of water. "Nothing would come from your well . . . only a little rust. So many of the wells in Rio Blanco are going dry."

She put a small amount of water in the shaving mug and started to stir with the brush.

"Aren't you gonna sharpen that razor?" he asked. "Hand me that damn strap and I'll do it. Can't shave with a dull blade, woman."

Despite his gruff tone, Consuelo got up and took down the leather strap. Tom tried to set up a little higher on his pillows, wincing with every movement until he finally gave up and fell back out of sheer exhaustion.

"I'm weak as a kitten," he grumbled, wondering why the peyote in the soup refused to work.

Without waiting for further instructions, Consuelo began mopping soap lather over his whiskers. Then she started honing the razor back and forth until she was satisfied with the edge.

"Lie still," she said softly, beginning with the razor high on Tom's right cheek. "I don't wish to cut you . . ."

"Like hell you don't," Tom replied. "You'd like nothin' better than to slit my throat."

The blade scraped through his whisker stubble on his cheeks and chin. As Consuelo went to work on his neck, he watched her closely from the corner of his eye, fearing a mortal stroke across his neck. Soon the shaving was done and he hadn't felt a nick. She wiped the remaining soap off his face and smiled.

"You look better now," she said, folding his razor. "Tomorrow I will bring my scissors to trim your hair."

"I don't want it cut too damn short," he warned.

Once again she ignored him, getting up to toss out the shaving water. She started out of the room until he spoke.

"Bring me my guns," he said. "There's a little bottle of gun oil to the left of the stove. Bring the oil and a rag. Time I started cleanin' my guns for my appointment with Luis Valdez."

Consuelo looked over her shoulder. "No, Tom. I won't do it. I won't help you prepare your guns. You'll have to get them yourself." At that, she walked out of the bedroom before he could launch any form of protest in her presence.

"I asked you to bring me my goddamn guns an' that oil!" he shouted to an empty room. "I asked you real nice, woman! Just who the hell put you in charge around here?"

He got no reply. The back door slammed, then there was silence. A chicken squawked in the backyard, taking his mind off Consuelo's refusal briefly.

Minutes passed, and Consuelo did not return to the house. It was quickly apparent she had no intention of bringing him his .44 and his rifle. Summoning all his strength, he pushed up to a sitting position and inched his legs off the edge of the bed. "I'll get the goddamn guns myself," he growled, trying to shut out the bolts of pain shooting through his side. When his feet touched the floor he took a deep breath and attempted to stand. Suddenly the floor tilted underneath him. Flashing pinpoints of light began to swim at the edges of his vision. He knew he was falling and tried to catch himself with a palm to the top of the nightstand, then everything went dark and the pain was gone.

Chapter Nine

By lantern light, he watched Maria carry his clean nightshirt and a pair of faded denims to the wardrobe closet on the far side of the room.

"How are you feeling today, Señor Tom?" the girl asked.

"Like a rusty bucket with a hole in it," he answered. His gaze was drawn to the swell of Maria's breasts. Her flour-sack dress clung to her skin in the stifling midsummer heat, leaving nothing to the imagination. The girl hung his clothes and turned around. She took notice of Tom's stare and smiled.

"They are bigger," she whispered, as though she shared a secret with him now. She threw her shoulders back to make her point.

"They damn sure are," he replied hoarsely, with a tone of wonderment. "Growin' faster'n weeds in the spring."

Maria skipped playfully over to his bed, still jutting her chest under his admiring glances, turning this way and that to give him a better view. But when she saw the old bloodstains on his bedsheet and the bandage, she stopped posing for him and frowned. "So much blood," she exclaimed, clasping a palm over her mouth. *"Madre!* I know you must have terrible pain, Señor Tom."

"It still hurts some," he replied, no longer staring at her breasts, for her face was prettier than he remembered it, thus he stared at it for a while. "I'm trapped in this damn bed, Maria, so I need a favor from you. Run in the other room and fetch my pistol and rifle. There's a little bottle of gun oil by the stove. Find me a rag someplace, too, so I can clean my guns while I can't do much of anything else."

Maria scurried out of the bedroom, passing between Tom and the lantern. He couldn't help but notice the slight rounding of her hips silhouetted inside her thin dress. "If Arturo'd only listen to me," he muttered under his breath. "Maria would draw lots of customers to his place, pretty as she is now . . ."

She returned with his cartridge belt slung over a shoulder, his Winchester requiring both her hands. When she placed his weapons on the mattress beside him she said, 'I'll hurry back with the oil and cloth."

He looked deeply into her chocolate eyes before she turned away, somewhat surprised when the sight stirred him. A warm sensation spread through his groin in spite of the nagging pain from his injury. It had been so long since he'd felt an urge that he failed to recognize it until the girl left the room. "Damn," he whispered, as the warm feeling intensified. "She sure as hell ain't no little girl anymore."

Maria came back with the oil and rag. She smiled when she gave them to him, allowing her hand to touch his longer than necessary, her face bent very close to his. But then she noticed the blood again and straightened up quickly, her mood changing abruptly to one of seriousness.

"Tomorrow night, I can give you a bath, Señor Tom," she said, "and change your bedsheet, if you wish. You should not be lying in a bed with so much blood. My mother will wash everything. There is dry blood all over your shirt . . ."

He caught himself thinking lecherous thoughts and quickly pushed them aside. "It wouldn't be proper for a girl to give a man a bath, Maria. I'm obliged for the offer, but . . ."

She adopted a pouty expression, lifting her chin. "I am not a girl any longer, Señor Tom. I am a woman now. Remember? When I showed you?"

"I remember it real well," he replied thickly, turning his face to another part of the room. "But it still wouldn't be the proper thing for a young lady the likes of you. Consuelo can give me a bath when she comes back tomorrow. She's seen everything there is to see when a man takes off his clothes."

"She told me . . . about what men are like," the girl responded in a silky voice. "She told me how to touch a man in the right places, to make him . . . ready for a woman."

Tom made a face. "The bitch hadn't oughta be tellin' you those things. You've got lots of time to learn on your own, damn her!"

Maria's smile returned, then she lowered her voice even more. "I touched Carlos Diaz the way she showed me. Carlos said it felt very good. He wanted me to do more, but I told him that I would only do more for money. Carlos and his family are very poor, like our

103

family. He had no money to pay me, and he called me bad names when I would not touch him again.''

"That's what I'm talkin' about,'' Tom explained, gratified that she had made his point for him. "A whore gets called every name in the book, Maria. You've got no business in the whorin' profession. You'd make somebody a real nice wife . . .''

She was shaking her head back and forth before he could finish. "Then I would still be poor,'' she said, "with many children and a poor husband who has nothing but a few sheep. A *puta* owns fine dresses and silk stockings, pretty corsets covered with lace, and leather shoes with high heels. Even many parasols, all different colors, and hats with beautiful feathers and fine shell combs for their hair. Bright ribbons, too. So many wonderful things. I will never be a man's wife, Señor Tom. I am tired of being poor!''

"You've let Consuelo poison your mind,'' he answered back. "It ain't all true, what she told you. Just look at her. She's poor as a church mouse . . . no fancy dresses or things like that. She's nothin' but a used-up whore, fat as a pot-lickin' dog, and she ain't got a grain of good sense in her empty head. You hadn't oughta listen to her. She ain't tellin' you all of the truth.''

Maria turned for the bedroom door. "My mind is made up,'' she said, glancing backward. "As soon as I can save enough money, I will go to Laredo to become a *puta*. Nothing you say can make me change my mind. *Buenas noches,* Señor Tom.''

He listened to the sounds she made leaving the house, then he let out a sigh. It was pointless to argue with her. Her family's poverty would drive her to one of the larger towns to escape the hopelessness of life in Rio Blanco, now that her head was full of sugarplum notions about the life of a whore. She had Consuelo to thank for that.

He put Maria out of his mind to examine his guns. Slowly, his hand closed around the butt of the Colt .44. It came from the leather holster easily. For a time he simply stared at it, feeling its heft in his palm. "I had the bastard in my sights," he said later, remembering the duel with Valdez. "Bad luck is all it was, to be ridin' that gun-green stud when the shootin' started."

He thumbed open the loading gate. Two spent shells gave off a dull gleam in the lantern light. He rodded them out on the mattress, barely noticing the musical tinkle of empty brass. Then he spun the cylinder, listening to the rhythmic click of the mechanism with his thumb lifting the hammer slightly. He knew the sounds and the feel of the Colt intimately. For more years than he cared to count, it had been the tool of his trade.

Pouring a spot of oil onto the cloth, he began to wipe down the Colt's surfaces, until the gun glistened. A small amount of oil was applied to the walnut grips, then he was satisfied.

It required more effort to oil his rifle. Working the ejection lever pained him. He inspected the firing chamber and reloaded after he'd given the Winchester a thorough oiling. Exhausted, he knew he'd lost track of time.

When he rested his head on the pillows to close his eyes, something Consuelo said echoed through his mind. It was true, he had fired two shots at Valdez and both of them missed. Was it possible that his eyes were actually going bad on him? Could that be the reason he'd allowed the Mexican to outgun him?

"I just know it was that damn horse's fault," he whispered, lost in a recollection of the exchange of gunfire.

Thus reassured, he drifted off into an uneasy sleep, awakening often throughout the night in a cool sweat that seemed to cling to his skin like oil.

Benito entered the bedroom with his straw sombrero in his hands. He halted a few feet from the bed and put on his best smile. "I fed your horse every day," he said, addressing Tom with a touch of concern in his voice that did not match the look on his face. Then his smile faded. "But now, there is no water for the bay. Your well has gone dry. This morning, there was nothing no matter how long I pumped."

"Consuelo told me," Tom replied, wondering what he would do. It sometimes helped to replace the sucker rod leathers, but there was no way he could perform the task in his present condition. "Maybe new leathers would help. Did you remember to prime it, Benito?"

Benito nodded quickly. "With water from my own well, señor. For a few more days, I will take water to your horse from my own well, but it too gives only a small stream. Very soon, I fear it will also be dry and there will be no water for my family, or for my chickens."

Tom's face darkened. "While we're on the subject of chickens, Benito, I wish the hell you'd do something to keep that red rooster from shittin' all over my yard. It wouldn't be very neighborly to shoot another man's rooster, but I've been damn close to it lately. I get shit all over my boots every time I go outside. Damn near slipped down the other day, and that's a fact. Maybe your wife will fix a special stew pretty soon. Boiled rooster makes a real good soup if you cook it long enough. Otherwise, I'll be forced to kill that red bastard. A man deserves some privacy around his own property, without slippin' and slidin' through piles of rooster shit every time he goes for a walk.''

Benito lowered his head and looked at the floor. "I am very sorry for the actions of the rooster," he said humbly, fingering the brim of his hat. "But if my wife makes soup with him, there will be no more chicks to replace my laying hens."

Hearing Benito's apology softened Tom's hard line on the subject for now. Benito was a neighbor. Other than the piles of chicken droppings, there had been good relations between them. "I reckon it'll keep," he said with less emotion. "If I had a dog that was worth the gunpowder it would take to kill him, he'd see to it that the rooster did his shittin' someplace else. I'm obliged for the loan of water for my horse. I'll see if I can find somebody to put new leathers on the rod. If that don't work, I don't know what I'll do, but I'll think of something."

Benito looked up. There was worry in his eyes. "More wells are going dry every day," he said. "Perhaps it is the will of God that we all leave Rio Blanco. Without water, no one can stay."

Tom wanted to sound bright and optimistic. "It'll rain one of these days real soon," he said. "It almost always rains in the fall, and then our wells will fill up again. The grass'll turn green and everybody will prosper. You gotta have faith in the seasons, Benito. It almost always rains in the fall.''

Benito left it unsaid that it had not rained in the fall for four years around Rio Blanco. Last year, there had been some promising showers near the end of September, but they ended abruptly and not a drop of water had fallen on the town since, Tom remembered.

"I hope your wound recovers quickly," Benito said. He started for the bedroom door. "I will tell my wife to chase the rooster from your yard with her broom," he added without looking back, then he went out on the porch and closed the door.

A cool morning breeze lifted the curtains in the bedroom, curtains Tom despised, a gift from Rosa that looked silly in a man's house with their little pink and blue flowers. The breeze felt wonderful and for a time he forgot about everything else, until he remembered the well.

"If that well's gone bone dry, I'll be in real trouble," he said under his breath. He'd been talking to himself a lot more lately. "If I can't water my horse or boil a pot of coffee when the goddamn store's got some beans, I'll have to move. Don't know where the hell I'll go . . ."

The black prospect of moving to another town was about the worst fate he could imagine. The cattle could stay so long as the pool held out, but if those springs dried up, too, he'd be ruined. Cattle buyers from San Antone were paying twelve dollars a head for longhorns, according to Hank. He wouldn't have enough left over at twelve a head to make a fresh start, and he'd never be able to sell his deeded acres if there was no water or grass. "I'll be wiped out," he added to his ruminations. To take his mind off his dark mood, he examined his guns again, this time in daylight. It felt better to have his weapons on the bed beside him, though he couldn't put a finger on the reason.

Half an hour later, while he was dozing, he heard a horse trot up to the front of the house. Peering out a window, he saw Chap Grant dismount and tie off his horse to a porch post. Chap's boots clumped to the door.

"C'mon in, Chap," he said in the loudest voice he could manage.

Chap entered the bedroom, wiping trail chalk from his face and neck with a soiled bandana. "I see you're lookin' like a man who expects to live," he observed, a one-sided grin lifting a corner of his mouth. "Some of us wouldn't have paid much for your chances."

Tom's cheeks hardened. "I ain't all that easy to kill. Folks around here oughta know that by now. Valdez got off a lucky shot. Every now an' then, the best gambler gets a bad turn of the cards."

Chap put his bandana away in a back pocket. "Four of those missing cows belong to you," he said. "Chance lost three. The rest are mine."

Tom decided it was time to give the rancher a stern lesson in business practices. "There's your profit for the year, Chap. The way I see it, you ain't got much choice. You and Chance need to strap on the guns and go down to Mexico to get your cows back."

Chap's face lost some of its color. "I'm not a gun-fighter, Tom. Neither is Chance. We could get shot full of holes. I've got a family to raise an' so does Chance. Those Rangers promised they'd look into the affair with the *comandante* over in Guerrero. Maybe they can get our cattle back."

"A waste of time," Tom replied, making a face. "There's just one way to do it. Ride down there an' stick your guns in their direction. A *bandido* understands flyin' lead better'n anything else."

Chap looked askance, unable to meet Tom's level

gaze. "I reckon we'll let the law take care of it. I just wanted you to know how many of 'em was yours."

Tom rested a hand atop the stock of his rifle. Chap's eyes followed the motion until Tom spoke. "As soon as I can sit a horse, I'm going' down there to take back my cattle and square things with Luis Valdez. If you boys want to ride along, you'll be welcome. But I damn sure won't let any of my cows become permanent residents of Mexico."

Chap squirmed uncomfortably. "You're gonna be laid up for a spell," he said, changing the subject. "I asked Jesus to get off a wire to the doctor in Laredo when he sent for the Rangers. You need to have a sawbones look at that bullet hole. When the freight wagon came last week, it brought a message from Doc Guthrie. He said he'd be over as quick as he could to take a look at you, if you wasn't already dead by then."

"I'm a hell of a long ways from bein' dead," Tom said, disgusted by Chap's refusal to go after his missing cows. He'd been right the first time, figuring the rancher to be a coward. Tom was losing all respect for Chap this morning. It would serve him right if the rustling forced him out of business when his notes came due in the fall. "I've got bigger problems right now," Tom went on, knowing it was a waste to discuss the stolen beeves any longer with Chap. "My well's gone plumb dry. I figure new leathers will help. Ask Jesus to drop by the house the next time he's in town. I'll pay him to fix my pump, if you ain't needin' the boy's services some afternoon."

Chap's shoulders sagged. He let out a sigh. "I may not be able to keep Jesus much longer," he said sadly. "The way things are, I can't afford a hired hand through the winter."

"You'll be sellin' out, like Hank," Tom remarked, though he didn't give his reasons. In Tom's view, Chap wasn't fit to be a rancher in South Texas, not if he didn't have the stomach to go after his stolen property.

Chap shook his head, like there wasn't much argument about it. "I can't pay the bank what I owe, not with prices like they are, and nothin' but thin calves to sell. This drought is liable to be the end of me, Tom."

"It ain't just the drought," Tom began. "A man who ranches in this country has got to be as tough as the land he grazes, and when a pack of owlhoots steals from him, he's got to have the backbone to go after what's his and take it back."

Now the rancher's cheeks colored. "I never was much good with a gun. That Ranger captain said he'd do everything he could, so I reckon I'll leave it to the law."

"You'll starve," Tom stated flatly, looking away at nothing in particular.

"I'd better be going," he said, avoiding any further discussion about the missing cows. "I'll send Jesus over. Maybe first thing in the morning."

Chap turned on his heel and walked out of the bedroom. Tom found he couldn't look at the rancher just then, now that he had Chap pegged for a coward. He listened to the sounds as Chap mounted his horse and rode off. "You ain't fit to call yourself a cowman," he said later, after the last hoofbeat faded away.

Chapter Ten

Consuelo's eyes rounded when she saw the guns lying beside him. "How did you get them?" she asked, halting a few feet away with a bowl of soup steaming in her hands.

"That's none of your damn business," he replied coldly. "Could be I got up and got 'em all by myself. The chamberpot's full again, so before I try to eat what's in that bowl, it needs to be tossed out the back door. Stinks worse'n a pigsty in here."

Consuelo was still looking at the guns, and now her eyes were flashing with anger. "If you got the guns yourself, you can carry the pot to the back door also." She looked at him. "Ask me to do things for you in a nice way, Tom. I made this *fríjoles* soup for you, because we are friends, and now you talk to me this way."

"That pot stinks," he answered back. "Besides, you started things off on the wrong foot by refusing to bring me my guns yesterday. It was just a little favor, an' you balked like some overloaded mule."

The look on her face softened some, then she approached the bed and gave him the soup. "I will empty the pot," she said with a sigh, bending down to pick it up, her nose wrinkling at the smell. She wouldn't look at him when she started out of the room.

"Thanks for the soup," he muttered. "If you'd brought me my guns like I asked you to, I'd have been in a better mood."

She halted near the door frame, being careful not to spill the contents of the pot. "I was hoping you would not carry a gun anymore," she said quietly.

Tom set his jaw. "As long as I'm breathin', I'll have a gun tied to my waist. Some folks around here have gone yellow, but I damn sure ain't gonna be counted amongst 'em. When a man ain't got the stomach to fight for what's his, he'd just as well go dig his own grave and lie down in it."

The fire was gone in Consuelo's eyes when he spoke. "No one has ever doubted your courage, Tom. That bullet almost ended your life. It is only because I . . ." She didn't finish, going through the door instead, leaving him to wonder.

He tasted the bean soup and found it delicious. "The woman knows how to cook," he said to himself. "I suppose that's how she got so fat in the first place."

He heard the contents of the chamberpot splatter across the yard moments later, and the squawk of a chicken in flight which brought a smile to his face. "Maybe if the red bastard has to dodge enough of my piss he'll go someplace else."

When Consuelo returned, he gave her the makings of a smile. "I like the soup," he told her.

She settled into the chair beside his bed. For a time

she simply watched him eat. He noticed that she was wearing red ribbons in her hair today, and that her face looked freshly scrubbed despite the heat in the room. Once, he took a sideways glance at the cleft between her breasts where the low neckline of her blouse left her bare.

"It is time to change the bandage," she said, halting the spread of warmth in his groin. "I brought clean strips of cloth, and more of the peyote pulp. The bedsheet must also be washed."

"Maria said she'd do it," Tom replied. "Her mother's been doin' my laundry for years."

"Maria is a beautiful girl," she said, and the remark reminded Tom of the thoughts Consuelo had been planting in Maria's head.

"Stop tellin' that child she oughta be a whore," he growled, as he gave Consuelo an angry stare. "You've damn near ruined her with all that talk about whorin'. It's all she thinks about now."

Consuelo straightened in her chair. "She does not want to be poor all her life!" she protested. "For her, it is the only way to leave this terrible place. She wants more than life can give her in Rio Blanco."

"She ain't but sixteen. Fillin' her head with fancy ideas about the whorin' profession goes against the scripture. Hell, she's hardly more'n a child. Let her make up her own mind. Besides, livin' in Rio Blanco ain't all that bad."

Consuelo lowered her face to the floor. "I was only fourteen when I left Sabinas for the *puta's* cribs. We had nothing to eat. My father could not grow enough corn to feed all of us." A tear crept to the corners of her

115

eyes. "I did the only thing I could. We had no money. I remember we were always hungry."

"You've been eatin' pretty good lately," he said, still angry at what she was doing to Maria. He looked at Consuelo, her generous bosom, the rounding of her belly. "You ain't missed any meals that I can tell."

The remark stung Consuelo . . . she got up quickly, with more tears flooding her cheeks. *"Bastardo!"* she hissed, wheeling away from the bed. She hurried out of the room, then he heard the front door slam.

The crunch of her sandals halted not far from his porch. He was puzzled, and turned his head to see out the front window. Consuelo was standing in his front yard, looking at the house.

"Bastardo!" she screamed with all her might. *"Bastardo!"* she cried again.

Her voice would carry all over Rio Blanco, he knew. Delia Cummings would be racing out her back door to see what the ruckus was all about. Gossip about the incident would spread like a prairie fire all over town by the time Delia was done with it.

He cupped his hands around his mouth, though it pained him to move his arms so quickly. "Get the hell outa my yard!" he shouted at the top of his lungs. "What the hell does a whore know about takin' care of a sick man!"

As proof of his earlier prediction, he heard Delia Cummings's rear door slam shut and he knew she was standing on her back porch with an ear cocked toward the disturbance. He fell back against the pillows and closed his eyes. "I'm gonna build that goddamn fence this fall," he promised himself. "I'll fence off the whole damn yard!"

A further annoyance arrived a few minutes later, while he was dozing. He awakened to clucking sounds outside a bedroom window and he knew Benito's rooster had come back. In his mind's eye, he saw hundreds of slippery deposits scattered across his yard. His right hand moved to the stock of the Winchester. If he could only sit up and hobble to the window, he would make good on his threat to kill the wandering chicken. The gunshot would bring everyone in Rio Blanco and he'd have to explain. Some might wonder if he'd lost his mind, shooting a tiny rooster with a big bore rifle. Thus he abandoned the idea and closed his eyes again, forced to endure the constant clucking and the knowledge that piles of droppings accompanied the sounds.

Maria entered the house. She carried a wooden bucket of water into the bedroom, with a clean linen for his bed draped over her arm. She smiled and placed the bucket beside the bed. 'I have come to give you a bath,'' she said.

Tom's eyebrows knitted. "It ain't hardly proper," he reminded her. "I told you I'd get Consuelo to do it."

She reached for the buttons on his nightshirt, and now her smile was gone. "Consuelo sent me," she said, opening the top button, then the next, despite his objections. "She has sworn never to come back to this house, Señor Tom. You made her very angry. She told my papa there would be snow in July before she ever came here again. I have a clean sheet for the bed, and cloth for bandages. Papa knows I am here. He gave his permission for the bath."

The news that Pedro approved of the task his daughter

was about to undertake left Tom momentarily speechless. A sixteen-year-old girl had no business washing a naked man. "Damn that Consuelo," he muttered, as the last button was opened on his nightshirt.

"I will help you sit up," Maria offered. "If you can stand for only a few moments, I will change the linen first."

"I'll be naked," he protested, as she took his right arm to assist him to a sitting position. He sat up with no small amount of effort and slowly moved his legs off the mattress until his feet touched the floor. The nightshirt slipped off his shoulders and fell to his waist, revealing the blood-encrusted bandage over his wound.

"I have seen naked men before," Maria assured him. "Now, see if you can stand up. It will only take a minute to change the sheet."

With her help, he stood up on unsteady legs and held on to an edge of the nightstand. The nightshirt fell to the floor around his ankles. He felt keen embarrassment when he looked down at his shriveled genitals. Maria hurried to removed the blood-stained sheet, hardly seeming to notice his plum-colored testicles. Razor-sharp pains went up and down his left side, but he managed to stand and took it as encouragement that he would soon be able to walk.

"The bed is ready," Maria said. She took his arm and helped him to sit down on the mattress. "Lie down now, and I will wash you," she added.

He looked up at her. "I'd just as soon you didn't," he said. "It don't seem natural. Put some water in that pan and I'll do it myself."

"Don't be silly," she scolded, as he lay back against

the pair of pillows. The bed frame squeaked until he was settled on the mattress, then he covered his privates with a hand, making Maria giggle.

"What's so damn funny?" he asked scowling.

Her face grew serious. "Nothing, Señor Tom," she answered, wetting a piece of cloth. She began to wipe the rag over his skin, first his shoulders, then his chest. When she came to the bandage, she put the cloth in the bucket and untied the knots in the strips of bedding. She was able to get the old bandage off without hurting him, then she tossed it to the floor and started to clean away the dried blood.

He looked down at the hole below his rib cage. A scab had formed around the opening. He'd been lucky. The bullet somehow missed his vital organs and exited through his back. With his hand covering his genitals, he allowed Maria to clean the wound and tie new strips of cloth around him. But when she resumed bathing the rest of his body, he halted her hand. "I'll do that part," he said, taking the damp rag himself. "I'd be obliged if you'd turn your head while I go about it."

Her smile angered him, though she did turn around as he'd asked. He hurried to wash his privates, feeling color rise in his cheeks. "There," he said, finished. "Now hand me that clean nightshirt you brought yesterday. And when you're done helpin' me into it, go fetch that bottle of whiskey in the kitchen."

She went to the wardrobe and brought him the shirt. He got it over his head without too much pain and effort. Now properly clothed, he felt much better, although the strain of so much movement left him weak. The pains started to ease before Maria came back with the bottle

119

and a glass. She poured him a generous shot and placed the bottle on the nightstand.

"There's a little money in the sugar bowl on the kitchen table," he said. "Pay yourself twenty-five cents and take twenty-five cents more to your mama, to pay for the laundry. That blood'll be hard to wash out." Then he thought of something else. "You come back tomorrow an' fix me somethin' to eat, dump out the chamberpot an' see to that damn worthless dog. We'll make it a regular job 'til I can get up and around. I'll pay you four bits a week. That way you'll have some spendin' money."

Maria's face was bright with anticipation. "I can save it for the trip to Laredo!" she exclaimed. "I already have thirteen pennies and a shiny silver *peso!*"

He took a big swallow of whiskey. "Wish you'd use the money for somethin' else," he said. "Goin' off to learn the whorin' profession ain't such a good idea."

"I am going," she replied evenly, with resolve in her voice. "I will not change my mind."

He drank again, when he could think of nothing else to say. It was clear that her mind was made up. "Somebody oughta cut off Consuelo Gomez's tongue," he said a moment later.

Maria picked up his soiled laundry, then the bucket, and started for the door. "I will come back tomorrow," she said, pausing at the lantern to turn down the wick. *"Buenas noches,* Señor Tom. *Adiós."*

He waved to her as she left the room. Later, he heard her open the sugar bowl and count the money. When she left the house he poured more whiskey and rested his head on the pillows to drink, watching shadows dance

120

on the bedroom wall as currents of air made the tiny flame flutter inside the lamp globe.

"Won't be long 'til I'm able to walk," he told himself. "A week more and I'll be able to ride. Best you learn to sleep with one eye open, Valdez. 'Cause I'm comin' for you, soon as I can sit a horse. You'll get one more chance to kill me, you thievin' Mexican bastard. But you'd better be quick the next time. I won't miss when we face each other again . . ."

Chapter Eleven

Captain Hardin swung a leg over the rump of his grullo gelding and dismounted. Tom examined the good mouse-colored horse from his rawhide chair on the porch. The Ranger apparently understood the value of tough horses in rough, dry country. The grullo's breeding showed.

"I see you're out and about," Hardin said, climbing the porch steps with saddle-weary legs that Tom knew from experience of his own.

"Movin' kinda slow," Tom replied. It had been five days since the Rangers departed for Guerrero. "But I'm healin', I reckon."

Hardin entered the shade and slouched against a porch rail. He had something on his mind, judging by his actions.

"Did you find those cows?" Tom asked, even though he was sure he already knew the answer.

The captain wagged his head. "Had a talk with Comandante Ortega over in Guerrero," he said, dawdling over the words, as though he was choosing them carefully. "It didn't amount to much."

"I tried to tell you," Tom reminded. "Be the same as talkin' to a dead man if you was tryin' to get anything done. Did you deliver my message to Luis Valdez?"

"Nope," the captain answered, hooking his thumbs in his gunbelt. "I was sorta hopin' you'd changed your mind."

"Billygoats will sprout wings before I change my mind about killin' that son of a bitch," Tom snapped, looking Captain Hardin in the eye.

"Too bad," Hardin said, without any real feeling. He gave Tom a look of appraisal. "Nothin' wrong with a feller havin' pride in my book," he added, "but it can get in the way sometimes. Comes a time when a man has to swallow his pride now and then. This is liable to be one of those times, T.C."

"Maybe," Tom replied with a shrug. "But I never was the kind who'd tuck tail and run. The bastard stole my cows. Makes twice he's done it now. That earns him a dose of hot lead in this part of the country. I'm gonna deliver it, soon as I'm able."

Hardin grunted, as though he understood. "Lead flies in different directions, sometimes. You're wearin' the proof with that hole in your side."

"He got lucky," Tom answered quickly, remembering that he'd explained it once before. "Even a blind hog finds an acorn every now and then. Valdez don't know it yet but his luck just ran out. He shoulda killed me when he had the chance."

The captain cast a roving glance toward Rio Blanco, then he fixed his gaze on Tom. "Valdez is good with a gun," he said. "I ran across Captain Hollaman down in Zapata a couple of days ago. Hollaman's retired now, but he remembered Luis Valdez. He told me he'd never seen a feller any quicker on the draw."

Tom remembered Travis Hollaman, from his days as commander of the Texas Ranger Post at Laredo. "I knew Trav Hollaman. It was a while back. We had our differences back then. I had a scrape or two with the law in my time."

"He told me," Hardin recalled. "He said he never could hang anything on you . . . he remembered that. He asked me to give you a message, T.C. Said it was for old time's sake. He said you ought to ride clear of Luis Valdez. He figures Valdez is faster."

Tom stiffened in his seat. "I reckon he's got a right to his opinion. I aim to prove otherwise, as soon as I'm able to travel."

Hardin shrugged again. "It don't really make no difference to me, so long as it don't happen on this side of the border. Just thought I'd pass along what Captain Hollaman said, in case you was interested."

"Well, I ain't," Tom said with heat in his voice.

The captain pushed away from the porch rail. "I figured as much," he replied absently. "Time I started back, T.C." He twisted one end of his handlebar mustache, as though it was merely something to do with his hand. "I sent my deputy upriver yesterday, to see if he could find any cattle tracks making a crossing. Word is that Luis Valdez is back in the rustling business. We've had more reports of stolen cattle east of here. With a piece of luck, maybe we'll catch him on this side of the border with a herd."

Captain Hardin went down the steps to his horse. Tom watched him mount, then he gave the Ranger a wave.

"Be seein' you, T.C.," Hardin said, then he wheeled

his grullo and roweled the horse to a trot away from the house.

Rosa came outside, shading her eyes from the sun to watch the Ranger depart. "I am finished with the sweeping, Señor Tom," she said a moment later. "There is no water, so the dishes are not washed."

Tom was forced to remember the unsuccessful attempt Jesus made to get the pump going. New leathers did nothing to bring water to the pump jack. "I'll borrow some," he said tiredly. "I'll ask Maria to fetch some when she comes for my laundry." He scowled at the front yard. "You didn't sweep today. I can see droppings."

"El gallo," she said under her breath. "Benito's rooster has come back. I swept the yard this morning . . ."

"I'm gonna have to kill that chicken," he said ruefully, though he knew he would secretly enjoy it. "I talked to Benito about it and he promised he'd do everything he could."

He signaled for Rosa to help him out of the chair. For the past three days he'd been able to struggle into his denims and boots to walk out on the porch in the evening. Being confined to his bedroom had almost driven him mad lately, thus the need to change his surroundings. He came slowly to his feet, grimacing when the effort stretched the healing around his wound. "I can make it now," he told her, then he hobbled to the front door and went in.

Rosa followed him into the bedroom to pull off his boots, a task he could not accomplish without excruciating pain. He sat on the edge of the bed until she got his boots off.

"Shall I come back tomorrow?" she asked, when his

boots stood beside the wardrobe. "There is so little to do . . ."

He hadn't wanted to end Rosa's employment, even though it cost him only ten cents a week. But with Maria doing his cooking and the laundry, he had little need for Rosa now. Rosa had been working for him for years . . . he could not remember exactly how long. He looked at her for a moment, noticing for the first time that she had streaks of gray in her hair. "I reckon not," he said quietly, hoping to handle things as gently as he could. "Until I can figure a way to get some water, there ain't much you can do around here."

Rosa nodded, to say she understood. She bowed her head slightly and walked out of the room, then he heard her footsteps on the porch.

"Damn," he whispered, wishing he could have spared Rosa's feelings a bit more. He poured himself a shot of bourbon and knocked it back on his tongue. Outside, he heard the red rooster cackle and the sound made him flinch.

He lay back on the pillows to stare at the ceiling. It seemed that almost everything was turning sour all at once. His well was dry and he was still bedridden, more or less. His cattle were starving without grass and there was no water for his horse unless he borrowed it. Luis Valdez had stolen his saddle and bridle when he took the stud, and Benito Sanchez's rooster was still shitting all over his yard. Making matters worse, he was nearly out of Kentucky whiskey and he would be forced to drink Arturo's tequila until the next freight wagon came with his whiskey order. "Hard to figure how things could be much worse," he said aloud.

Events had taken a downward turn the day Luis Valdez showed up, thus the blame could rightfully be placed on his shoulders. While Valdez couldn't be faulted for the four dry years around Rio Blanco, he had a share in the rest of Tom's ills. "He's bad luck," Tom told himself, his gaze drifting to the gun belt hanging from a bed post at the foot of the bed. "When I kill him, it'll put an end to all this misfortune," he added. "Maybe it'll even rain."

Thus he made up his mind to tie on his gun tomorrow morning and begin a little target practice. The gunshots would draw the attention of everyone in town and most certainly irritate Delia Cummings, but it was high time he started preparing himself for the ride down to Guerrero. He wanted to test his aim, and his reflexes, to prove to himself that Consuelo had been wrong about his poor eyesight. He put no stock in the Ranger captain's message from Trav Hollaman that Valdez would be quicker at the draw. Hollaman would be eating those words when he learned that Tom had bested Valdez in a gunfight.

The sounds of an approaching horse took his mind off the coming duel. When he looked out the window, he saw Jessie Kootz ride up to the porch on his sweat-caked chestnut gelding. Tom had offered Jessie a dollar a week to keep an eye on his cows until he was able to do it himself. It was only temporary employment and Jessie understood. It was a chance for Jessie to stay in Rio Blanco a while longer, putting off his departure to look for a cowboying job someplace else.

Jessie clumped heavily across the porch and entered without knocking. He stuck his head around the door frame and gave Tom a toothless grin. "You've got your britches on," he said.

Tom waved Jessie into the room. "There's still a little whiskey, Jess," he said, aiming a thumb at the bottle. "How're my cows?"

Jessie walked stiffly to the nightstand and poured himself a drink in a smudged glass. "Thin," he answered, a needless observation during a drought. "That brindle cow got stuck in the mud tryin' to get a drink. I had to toss my loop over her horns an' pull her out. She's weak, but I reckon she'll make it a while longer. That pool's damn sure dryin' up fast, Tom. It's all those damn *borregos* crowdin' out the springs."

Tom nodded. "I've learned to hate sheep this year," he said, watching Jessie gulp down the whiskey. "Never hated a dumb animal in all my life until now, but this dry spell taught me to hate the woolly bastards. Learned to hate red roosters, too."

Jessie arched one gray eyebrow, to say he didn't understand when he heard the remark about roosters. He poured himself another drink and gazed out the window, looking south. "This country's bone dry now," he said absently. "There ain't an animal on earth that can live out there much longer. If it don't rain, there'll be cattle carcasses piled high as a man's head. Chap's calves have sucked his cows down to skin an' bones. They won't be worth a pewter quarter come market time."

Hearing so much grim news all at once, Tom reached for the bottle and took a long swallow from the neck. "Ain't you got anything good to report, Jess?" he asked.

The old cowboy shook his head sadly. "Not a cloud in the sky all day. The damn rattlesnakes won't even come out to feed in daylight. Too damn hot for 'em, I reckon." He turned away from the window, looking Tom in the eye. "You'll have to sell mighty soon," he added, trying to make the warning sound gentle. "Your cows are gonna start dyin' any day now, Tom. Some of 'em's too weak to wander off lookin' for grass. I saw it happen up in Kansas Territory one time, while we was holdin' a big herd outside Newton. Back in '68, I believe it was. Cattle just lowered their heads and wouldn't move. Wasn't no grass for miles. Late one afternoon, they started dyin', one at a time. You could hear 'em fallin' down all night. By mornin', we'd lost nearly two hundred head. About that many died the next day."

Tom made a face. "I'd just as soon not hear about it, Jess. If you ain't got any good news to give me, then I'd be obliged if you cleared out so I can get some rest. Tomorrow mornin' I'm gonna start some target practice, to get ready for a showdown with Valdez when I can ride. All this talk about dyin' cattle is keepin' me from gettin' my rest."

Jessie placed the glass on the table. He made a half turn for the door, then he hesitated and made a study of Tom's face. "I'll go with you down there," he said quietly. "Made up my mind about it the other day, whilst I was ridin' the pastures. You get ready to go and I'll oil up my old six-shooter. There was three of them when they came to town that night. I can make the others dodge some lead while you go up agin' Valdez."

Jessie's offer caught Tom off guard. The old man's courage surprised him. "Why would you risk your life, Jess? They didn't steal any cattle from you?"

Jessie shrugged. "I suppose you could say I'm sidin' with a friend. We've known each other a long time. Nobody else around here aims to back your play, so I reckon it falls to me. Hell, Tom, I've lived here most of my life . . . called this place home. A feller who won't stand

130

up to be counted when friends are in trouble ain't much of a man, to my way of thinkin'. So you can count me in when the time comes. I can't see all that good anymore, but I can sling some lead in the bastards' direction. Just let me know when you're able to ride and I'll have my six-gun ready."

"I want you to know I'm grateful," Tom replied. It was a rare expression of feelings, coming from Tom. "You've got backbone, something that's damn scarce around Rio Blanco lately. But I'll manage the shootin' part myself, Jess. I wouldn't want a friend's death on my conscience. You can lend me a hand drivin' those cows back across the river after I take care of Valdez. I'd be obliged for your help with the herd."

"I can shoot, Tom," Jessie said, standing a little straighter than before, though his slender shoulders were still rounded and his back was permanently bent with age. "I ain't no professional shootist like you was, but I can handle myself decent enough. You give the word when you're able to go down to Guerrero. I'll side with you every step of the way."

Tom let the subject drop, merely nodding before Jessie walked out of the room. It took a lot of courage for the old cowboy to put his life on the line like that. Tom found that he had new respect for Jessie Kootz.

Jessie paused at the edge of the porch. He spoke to Tom through the bedroom window. "Yonder's a red rooster in your front yard," he said, pulling his hat brim low over his eyes to keep out the slant of a late day sun. "Is that the one you was talkin' about a while ago?"

"That's the one. Never hated a chicken 'til that bastard came along. Watch your step out there, Jess. You're liable to fall down an' break your neck."

Maria brought him a bundle of warm tortillas for his supper. She emptied the chamberpot and changed his bandage after giving the wound a thorough cleaning.

"The swelling is going away," she said, tying a fresh strip of cloth around his ribs. "Consuelo asked about the swelling."

"She's just bein' nosy," Tom complained. "What the hell does she care?"

Maria fluffed the pillows behind him. "She loves you, Señor Tom. She asks about you every day."

He gave the girl a dark look. "A whore don't love nothin' 'cept money," he growled. "You remember that. If you take up whorin' you'll wind up just like her. She can hardly wait 'til I'm well enough to pay her a call, if you know what I mean. You can tell her that hell will be froze solid before she sees any more of my money."

She bent over the bed and kissed his cheek. In the light from the lantern he couldn't help but notice how she filled out her dress.

"Buenas noches," she whispered, then she turned down the wick and closed the door softly behind her.

Chapter Twelve

The empty whiskey bottle rested on a mesquite stump. He remembered the day he cut down the tree almost twenty years ago to make a clearing for a second corral which he never got around to building. He measured the distance carefully, exactly thirty paces, then he turned around and squared himself to make the draw. His side was throbbing from all the exertion and his body was bathed in a cold sweat by the time he'd made all the preparations. Now he hunkered down in a battle-ready crouch with his right hand a few inches above the butt of his gun.

First, he tested the feel of the Colt in its holster, lifting it slightly, then dropping it back. It came easily from its leather berth, just the right amount of pull, but not too much to slow him down. He looked at the bottle with hooded eyelids. Morning sunlight struck the glass, making it shimmer. "I can see it plain as day," he whispered to himself, lowering his voice even though no one was watching him. "There ain't a goddamn thing wrong with my eyeballs."

A new wave of pain made him wince when he tightened the muscles in his right arm, but he ignored it and focused his attention on the whiskey bottle. Unconsciously, his lips drew back across his teeth in a snarl, for in the bottle's place he imagined the face of Luis Valdez, leering at him from the shadow of a sombrero. Slowly, his fingers curled, to be ready for the draw. "Now, you Mexican bastard," he hissed, clenching his teeth. "Go for your gun!"

His hand dipped and his fingers closed. A jerk of his arm brought the .44 flying upward in his grasp. His thumb cocked the hammer as a reflex . . . in the same fraction of a second, he aimed and fired. The gun roared, shattering the silence around Rio Blanco. Tom blinked as a wisp of blue gunsmoke curled in front of him. The sound of the shot echoed from the scrub live oaks and mesquites. A tiny puff of dust arose from the hardpan more than two hundred yards beyond the stump where the bottle sat, untouched by the bullet.

"Damn!" he spat, grinding his teeth. How could he have missed at thirty paces?

He heard a door close behind him. There was no need to turn around to see who it was. A pain shot through his chest like a bolt of lightning as he holstered the gun for another try.

"My Clarence always wore his spectacles when he went hunting," Delia said. "He couldn't hit the side of a barn without them. If you were aiming at that bottle yonder, there's reason to suspect you need spectacles, too, Tom."

A flash of sudden anger almost brought harsh words to the tip of his tongue. Biting down, he struggled to control himself until the anger passed. "I wasn't aimin' at the bottle yet,'' he said with as much calm as he could muster. "Just gettin' the feel of my gun, is all."

A pause in the conversation forced Tom to look over his shoulder, in the hope that Delia had gone back inside. But when he turned his head, he saw Delia standing on her back porch, tying her sunbonnet in place as though she meant to stay for a while. He noticed too that more townspeople had come outside to find the source of the noise. Mrs. Sanchez was clad in her apron, her hands and forearms dusted with tortilla flour, watching him from her backyard. He sighed and turned back to the stump. One thing he didn't need right now was an audience.

"A man shouldn't be too vain to wear spectacles if he needs them," Delia declared. "That's what I always said to Clarence. If you can't see, there's no point in going hunting without them, I said."

"If blindness can be caused by overworked ears," he said softly, "it explains why Clarence couldn't see."

"I didn't catch what you said, Tom," Delia remarked.

He shook his head in resignation, fixing his gaze on the bottle. "It was nothing, Miz Cummings," he muttered. "Just talking to myself."

"I dearly hope this disturbance won't last too long," she said, as he was crouching for another fast draw. "I usually take a nap in the middle of the morning."

He decided to ignore her. His practice was far more important than maintaining good neighborly relations just now. Eyes slitted, he tensed his arm and prepared for the moment when he drew. The bottle was in perfect focus . . . he was sure of it. He sent his hand toward the gun as quickly as he could, blanking his mind so that habit and years of practice would direct his movements.

His fist came up filled with iron. The Colt exploded, an earsplitting bang that crackled through the surrounding trees and brush. Again, a spit of caliche flew from the dry ground beyond the stump and his heart sank when he saw that he had missed a second time.

"I do believe I've got the feel of it now," he said loudly, so Delia could hear. 'No sense wastin' a bottle until I got this Colt sighted in on that clump of grass."

"You could have fooled me," Delia said. "I was sure you'd aim at the bottle this time."

"No ma'am," he replied, forcing polite words from his mouth in a last effort to keep peaceful relations. "Not 'til I was ready."

"I suppose it's understandable," she continued, "that you would need time to get back in shape after your injury. We'd all given you up for dead, Tom, until that dreadful scarlet woman down at the cantina nursed you back to health. I guess women like her can't be all bad."

He had reached the limits of his patience now. Taking a deep breath, he turned around. "I'm tryin' to practice here, Miz Cummings," he said, measuring each word. "I can't do it while you're jabberin' at me. I'd consider it a personal favor if you'd go back inside to take your morning nap right now."

The stare she gave him would have melted ice. "I declare," she said. "I was only trying to be neighborly. My, but you've turned surly in your old age! Good day, Mr. Culpepper! I was baking a peach pie for you this morning, however your rudeness has made me change my mind. I'd rather feed my pie to your lazy, good-for-nothing dog than give it to the likes of you!"

She turned on her heel and marched inside, giving her back door a heavy slam to punctuate her final remarks. Tom felt some satisfaction that he'd finally been able to get under Delia's skin. He turned back to the stump, filled with a new sense of purpose. Crouching, he set his jaw and clawed for the gun. In a single, fluid motion, he pulled, aimed, and fired.

The sounds of exploding glass followed the thunder of the Colt. A grim smile crossed Tom's face briefly. Shards tinkled musically around the base of the stump. He straightened, and shoved the .44 back in its holster.

It required all the strength he had to make the walk back to his doorstep. By the time he climbed to the porch, his limbs were trembling with fatigue. Deep inside, however, he felt better than he had in quite a spell.

Hank Wardlaw pulled the saddle off the sorrel mare's back and carried it into the shed. "Keep it long as you like, Tom," he said, sleeving sweat from his forehead after the saddle was put away. "I don't hardly need a saddle for extra hands now. Kinda sad, knowin' there ain't a cow left on the place."

Tom steadied himself against the corral fence. The walk to the barn drained him. "I'll see that it gets back, Hank. I appreciate the loan."

Hank was reading Tom's expression. "You're dead set on going?"

He shook his head. "Damn right I am. My side's healin' real nice. I'll be fit as a fiddle by the end of the week."

Hank rested a hand on Tom's shoulder. "Sure wouldn't want to see anything happen to you," he said.

"There ain't a soul in Rio Blanco who'd find fault with you if you didn't go. Those two Rangers can handle Valdez if he shows up around here again."

"There's a principle involved, Hank. A man can't keep his dignity if he lets somebody else defend his honor. That renegade Mexican stole my cattle . . . twice, and put this hole in my side. I couldn't look at myself in the mirror if I walked away from it."

Hank dropped his arm to his side. "I understand," he said quietly. He started for his horse. "By the way, I appreciate what you're doin' for Jessie. Hardest thing I ever did, lettin' him go. If it wasn't for this damn drought, I'd have kept him on." He put a boot in a stirrup and pulled himself over the saddle, then he leaned over to pick up the lead rope on the sorrel mare. "What'll you do if it don't rain, Tom?"

Tom gave the dry brushland around Rio Blanco a passing glance before he answered. "Hard to say. Sell off a few more head, I reckon. I figure it'll rain this fall. It damn near always rains in September and October."

Hank was kind enough to leave it unsaid that it hadn't rained in the fall for four years. He swung his horse away from the corral and gave Tom a lazy wave. "Take care of yourself," he said, as his bay struck a trot toward town.

Tom watched the rancher ride off, thinking how different Hank seemed lately. "This dry spell broke his spirit," he muttered, taking short steps away from the fence.

He reached the porch and climbed the steps without noticeable pain in his side. Each day, the pain grew less. He settled into his chair as a gust of hot wind blew across the porch. Squinting to keep the dust out of his eyes, he almost missed seeing the black buggy coming out of the dry riverbed, pulled smartly by a buttermilk roan trotter. The carriage canopy was layered with chalky dust. The driver pulled his horse to a halt just as Hank was riding past.

"Wonder who the hell that is?" Tom asked himself, watching Hank look over his shoulder, pointing to Tom's house.

The driver tipped his derby hat and slapped the reins over the roan's rump. Dust from the carriage wheels spiraled and bent sharply in the wind. Half a minute later the buggy came to a stop in front of the porch. A round-faced man wearing pork-chop sideburns climbed down from the carriage seat.

"You T.C. Culpepper?" he asked, dusting off the front of his split-tail frock coat and then his trousers. He reached underneath the buggy seat and withdrew a black leather bag.

"I am," Tom replied.

"I'm Doc Guthrie. Sorry to be so late getting over to see you, but I've been swamped. It's a two-day drive to Rio Blanco in the first place and I was further delayed amputating a gentleman's leg near Encinal. Worst case of gangrene I've seen since the war. Now show me your injury. I was told you caught a bullet a few weeks back. It'll have to come out, you understand."

"It passed clean through, Doc," Tom replied, struggling out of his chair. "Come inside. I've got a little Kentucky whiskey to cut the dust out of your throat."

They shook hands. Dr. Guthrie took out a handkerchief and mopped his face. "Haven't had any good whiskey in years," he said, following Tom through the door.

Tom showed his visitor to a chair, eyeing the bottle on the drainboard. A mere two fingers of whiskey remained. He brought the bottle to the table and placed it in front of the doctor. "No clean glasses," he said. "My well's been dry for a week . . . no way to wash anything. Sorry."

Dr. Guthrie hoisted the bottle and took a swallow. "Show me the wound," he said, smacking his lips. "Damn, that's good stuff. No such thing as decent whiskey in Laredo lately."

Tom opened his shirt and took it off, then he gingerly untied the knots in the bandage and removed it. The doctor leaned out of his chair to peer into the wound, then he examined the hole in Tom's back where the slug had exited.

"Healing just fine," he said absently. "Missed your heart by a couple of inches. It had the right angle to miss your ribs back there. I'd say you're a very lucky man, Mr. Culpepper. Lucky to be alive, at any rate. I imagine it was quite painful."

"It still hurts some, Doc, when I move around."

The doctor took another swallow of whiskey. "I'm not surprised. Whoever took care of you must have known something about medicine. There's no pus. I doubt if I could have done any better."

Tom was forced to remember Consuelo's role in his recovery, and the Indian medicine plant she applied to his wound. He decided against mentioning it to the doctor. "How soon can I ride a horse, Doc?" he asked.

Dr. Guthrie shrugged. "I'd give it another week or two, so there's less risk of bleeding. I'll leave you a jar of salve. It helps the skin grow back, and it's only a dollar." He opened his bag and took out a small glass jar that smelled of wintergreen.

Tom removed the doctor's money from his sugar bowl.

"No charge for the visit," Dr. Guthrie said, pocketing the coins. "This whiskey is payment enough. You'd be dead by now anyway, if you hadn't been given excellent care by someone else."

Tom hadn't wanted to hear that he owed Consuelo his life. He tried not to think about her at all. "Maybe I was just lucky," he said.

The doctor stood up and closed his bag. "I'd say it was more than luck, Mr. Culpepper. Most men die of gutshot wounds. Gangrene sets in and then there's nothing anyone can do." He turned and started for the door. "Get plenty of rest, Mr. Culpepper. Use the salve every day. By the way, would you mind if I watered my horse before I start back?"

Tom followed the doctor outside. "I can't offer you any, Doc. My well's dry, like I told you. More than half the wells in this town have stopped giving water. Ask down at the cantina. Sorry I can't oblige."

Dr. Guthrie climbed into his buggy. "I understand. This is the driest country I've ever seen. On my way into town, I drove past a herd of longhorns that looked more dead than alive. Nothing but bones and horns. Whoever owns those cattle might as well call it quits. There won't be enough beef on them to make a bowl of stew."

The doctor waved and slapped the reins over his buggy horse, his grim pronouncement about the longhorns still ringing in Tom's ears. Were his cattle as thin as those the doctor described? Since the day before the shootout with Valdez, he had not seen his own herd and had only

Jessie's word about their condition. Now that he had a borrowed saddle, he could manage a ride down to the pool at the bend in the river to have a look for himself, though now he dreaded what he would find.

"I'll ride down there tomorrow morning," he promised himself as he walked back into the house. "It can't be as bad as the doc says."

Chapter Thirteen

He held the bay to a walk, to keep the horse's gait from worsening the pain in his side. Jessie rode to Tom's right, scanning the brush for wandering cattle as they neared the river-bend pool. Without Jessie's help, he'd have never been able to saddle the bay. Just as troublesome as the nagging pain was a generalized weakness in his limbs. Even the simplest chore left him exhausted, making him wonder if he would ever get his strength back.

Tom examined the scant grasses they rode past, widely scattered clumps of short, sun-dried tufts of curly mesquite offering little more than a mouthful here and there. Even the cholla spines had lost some of their color, and the agave looked brittle, as if the leaves would snap off in the next gust of dry wind. Ocotillo stalks rose like fire-blackened skeletons against a pale morning sky. The ground where cattle trails wound through the brush had been beaten to a powder by countless hooves. With every footfall, their horses sent up little clouds of white dust that clung to the animals' legs like sifted flour. It wasn't yet ten o'clock and already the heat waves danced before their eyes, creating the illusion of silvery lakes in the distance.

"Yonder's a cow and calf, Tom," Jessie said, pointing at the brush before them. "I do believe it's Chap's good red cow. She had twins year before last, if you'll remember."

It was the first cattle they'd seen since leaving Rio Blanco and Tom wasn't quite prepared for the sight. A big red longhorn with better than a six-foot-horn spread stood in the shade of a mesquite tree nursing her calf. The old cow's hip bones jutted like tent poles underneath her hide. Tom could count every rib down her side. Her flanks were sunken in so badly they almost touched at her udder. The calf punched her bag hungrily with its nose, trying to force a few more drops of milk from its mother.

"Damn," Tom said, his inspection over. "That's the hollowest cow I ever saw in my life, Jess. There's more meat on a hummingbird."

The cow snorted when the horses drew near, lifting her tail in the manner of all wild longhorns when danger was close. Under better circumstance, the old cow would have trotted off in the brush to protect her offspring. Weakened by starvation, she simply stood there, snorting a warning and shaking her horns menacingly until the riders went past.

"There'll be dead cattle all over the place in a couple of weeks," Jessie said. "If I was you I'd quit worryin' about *bandidos* stealin' any more of my cows. Stealin' cattle as thin as these are would be a waste of time."

Off in the distance, Tom could see the darker line of green in the brush marking the springs where the river made a turn. He was sure more sad sights awaited them at the pool. "It's the principle of the thing, Jess," he replied. "It don't matter so much what another man steals. It's the idea that he stole it in the first place. You gotta stand up for what you believe in . . . you can't let some owlhoot push you, or take what ain't his. South Texas would be a better place if we killed all the thievin' sons of bitches who'd take another feller's cows and horses. That's the way it used to be. When you caught some gent red-handed with somebody else's property, you was within your rights to string him up at the closest tree."

Jessie nodded. "It was simpler back then," he agreed, guiding his chestnut around a bed of prickly pear. "Now there's all them regulations havin' to do with the border. Hell, it ain't nothin' but a shallow river to begin with. In places, a feller won't get his knees wet makin' a crossing in the fall of the year."

Tom had all but forgotten about his wound until the bay stumbled over a rock in the trail. Wincing, he bent over in the saddle and waited for the sensation to pass. His attention was quickly drawn to other things when the horse rounded a turn, giving him a view of the bend in the riverbed. The pool had shrunk to half its size the last time he was here. Yellow mud, pitted with deep cattle tracks, completely encircled the waterhole now. On the east side, mired in belly-deep mud, lay the half-eaten carcass of a longhorn. A black buzzard was perched atop the cow's skull, tearing flesh from the exposed vertebra of the neck. Another vulture hopped clumsily to a better feeding spot in the cow's soft underbelly.

"Yonder's one to scratch off the tally book," Jessie said, standing in his stirrups for a better look.

Tom hoped they wouldn't find a Rafter C branded on the dead cow's flank. "She got bogged tryin' to reach

145

water," he said, even though Jessie didn't need an explanation.

Jessie turned his face to Tom. "It's fixin' to get a hell of a lot worse," he predicted, checking the sky for clouds needlessly, more out of habit than hopefulness.

On the far side of the bend, a few longhorns stood in the sparse shade of a mesquite thicket. Along the riverbank, a row of cottonwoods offered more shade where cattle rested, some with heads lowered near the ground, others lying down to chew their meager cud. "They're gettin' too weak to go off looking for grazing," Tom remarked. An odd tightness gripped his throat when he said it, as if the words wanted to stay inside his mouth.

"That's Chance's dead cow," Jessie offered, for now they were close enough to read the brand.

They rode to the slope in the riverbank leading down to the pool. Some of the longhorns on the far side came to their feet in cow-fashion, back legs standing first, then the front pair, the opposite of the way a horse came to its feet, forelegs first. It was something a cowman noticed.

"There's my brindle cow," Tom said softly, when he could see the animal's flank. Bitter bile rose in his neck. One of his best cows resembled a scarecrow. The calf standing at her shoulder looked to be about the size of a jackrabbit. As their horses started down to the pool, the buzzards beat their wings noisily into the air, driven off by the arrival of man-smell. Tom took his eyes off the brindle cow to watch the birds climb skyward. "They'll be the only things gettin' fat around here for a spell," he said, watching a vulture begin a slow circle above the pool, riding a current of air on outstretched wings.

"The way I see it, Tom, you're boxed in," Jessie said, slowing his gelding when it reached the mud. "You can't hold on much longer or you'll lose everything. When these cattle start dyin', there ain't no way to stop it 'til the last one falls. Same goes for the other ranchers around here. If it don't rain real soon, there won't be nothin' but bleached bones in these parts."

Tom let his horse navigate the mud to the edge of the pool. A horse was much stronger than a cow and wouldn't get stuck so easily. The bay lowered its head and started to drink, burying its muzzle below the surface as a good saddle horse should, a horseman's superstition that had always been reliable in Tom's experience. "I won't sell out, Jess," he said. "Remember what I said about havin' faith in the seasons. It damn near always rains in the fall. The Almighty plans it that way and I'll put my trust in the Lord."

Jessie gave him an odd look. "Didn't know you was a God-fearin' man, Tom."

"I dabble in a little bit of scripture now and then," he replied, sounding casual about it.

Jessie squinted thoughtfully across the pool. "I haven't seen the insides of a church house in quite a spell. We ain't had a preacher in Rio Blanco since Reverend Cummings passed away. I've tried to keep sinful notions out of my head and remember not to cuss on Sunday, but if there's anything to all that Bible verse, I figure I'm a doomed man. A cowboy's life is full of temptations. Maybe the Lord'll understand when I get to them pearly gates."

Tom remembered a few of Reverend Clarence Cummings's sermons, the few he attended. Delia played the foot-pump organ to accompany the gospel songs. The organ now sat in Delia's living room and on Sunday mornings she played a full hour of hymns with her windows flung open so everyone in town could hear. The organ music always triggered a concert of incessant braying from Pedro Flores's jackass on the other side of town, a further irritant when Tom had a hangover after a long Saturday night bout with whiskey, usually ending with a buck-jump at Consuelo's shack lasting until dawn. "I figure the Lord will make exceptions when it comes to cowboys," he said. "If He don't, hell is gonna be full of gents wearin' boots and spurs."

The bay lifted its muzzle, dribbling water on the surface of the pool. Tom reined toward the bank, unwilling to look across the river at his brindle cow and calf again, knowing that what he saw was sure to make him sad.

Jessie rode up beside him and glanced up at the sun. "Like a ball of fire," he muttered, "and it ain't even noon yet."

A sheep bleated from the brush before Tom could offer an opinion on the sun. Jessie's head turned toward the sound.

"There's the reason for half our troubles," he said, wagging his head sadly. "I quit wearin' wool shirts a few years back, on account it came from the hide of a goddamn *borrego*. I'd sooner freeze solid in the dead of winter than wear wool."

Tom said nothing on the subject, his mind elsewhere as they rode away from the river. His cattle were starving to death. If the dry spell lasted much longer, he wouldn't have a cow left to his name. The thought blackened his mood. "Let's head back, Jess," he said in a faraway voice. "I've seen enough for today."

His shipment of whiskey arrived, sparing his stomach from Arturo's firey tequila or worse, the golden mescal made down in Saltillo which was like swallowing a red-hot poker. Carlos Diaz brought Tom's whiskey in a pushcart and dutifully carried it into the house. Tom broke open one of the wooden crates, then uncorked a fresh bottle to sample it.

"Smooth as mother's milk," he said, handing Carlos a coin for the delivery.

The teenage boy bowed politely. *"Gracias,* Señor Tom."

It was then that Tom remembered what Maria told him. "That Maria Flores is a mighty pretty girl, ain't she?" he asked.

Carlos's coppery cheeks darkened with embarrassment. "She has a cold heart," he said. "She only thinks about money."

Tom had to suppress a laugh. "She hangs around with Consuelo Gomez too much. Money is the only thing Consuelo thinks about."

Carlos sighed. "All women are the same," he said, pocketing the coin as he made for the door. "Good afternoon, Señor Tom. It is good to see that you are feeling better."

When the boy was gone, Tom tipped up the whiskey and drank two big swallows. All afternoon, he had been in a dark mood over the condition his cattle were in. The prospect of going flat broke loomed larger now. Unless it rained soon, he would be finished in the cow business.

With the bottle in hand, he walked out on the porch

to sit and enjoy the cool of evening. His mind was made up to go after Valdez tomorrow night. Under the cover of darkness, he could slip into Guerrero unnoticed. This time, he would choose the meeting place for the duel. There wouldn't be a gun-shy horse underneath him to spoil his aim.

He drank again, to hurry the whiskey to his brain, thus to blot out recollections of the cattle they found at the river. He drew his shirt sleeve across his mouth, watching a late afternoon sun lengthen shadows across the brushland to the south. Tomorrow night, after he rested, he would ride that prairie to the Rio Grande, bent on killing a man, the man who had humiliated him and stolen his cows. Justice would be served, despite an international boundary. He would do what the Texas Rangers couldn't. He would take an eye for an eye.

The spotted dog nuzzled his hand, whimpering once. "What the hell do you want, you lazy bastard? As if I didn't know," he said, rubbing the dog's neck. He looked up at the sound of footsteps coming from town. Maria walked toward the house with a bundle in one hand. She waved when she saw him staring at her.

"Your supper," she said when she arrived, climbing the porch steps to give him a tin plate covered with a linen napkin. "Mama made tamales today. She said these were for you."

He could smell the delicious aroma before he took the plate, and likewise, the dog licked its lips hopefully. "Thank you, Maria," he replied, trying not to pay too much attention to the way her dress was clinging to her body. "Tell your mama I'm grateful. I'm needin' a good supper tonight. Tomorrow, I'm goin' after Luis Valdez.

With a bellyful of these delicious tamales, I can ride all the way to Mexico City if I have to.''

Worry wrinkled Maria's forehead. She waited until Tom took a drink of whiskey before she spoke. ''Consuelo told me you have been practicing with your pistol. No one in Rio Blanco wants to see you go to fight the *bandidos,* Señor Tom. Everyone would be happier if you stayed.''

He opened a corner of the napkin to sniff the contents of the plate. Rolled cornshucks were swimming in chili gravy below the cloth, making his stomach growl. ''I appreciate all the concern,'' he said, ''but there's a score to settle and I ain't the kind to hide behind a tree. I'm gonna kill that Mexican for what he done to me.''

She bent over him and kissed his cheek. ''Please be careful,'' she said softly. Bending over his chair, the front of her dress came open just enough to reveal the tops of her breasts.

He forced his eyes away from her bosom. One thing he didn't need right now was a distraction brought on by urges. ''I'll be real careful,'' he told her, looking at the tamales again to take his mind off other things. Remembering the delivery Carlos made, he decided to make another effort to reason with the girl about her future. ''I saw Carlos Diaz today,'' he said. ''He sure is a handsome boy. He'll make some lucky girl a good husband. He's a hard worker, too.''

The look on Maria's face told him of his failure before she said a word. ''He is only a little boy, and he will always be poor like his father. They have only a few sheep and goats, even less than my papa.''

He gave up on the notion that he could change her

mind. "You've been listenin' to Consuelo again, I see. Money ain't all there is to think about."

Her smile warmed him, and he forgot about everything else.

"Will you say goodbye to Consuelo before you leave tomorrow?" she asked.

"Hell no!" he replied quickly. "I've got nothin' more to say to that woman. She can't keep a civil tongue long enough to hold a conversation. Last time she was here, she stood out yonder in my front yard, callin' me a bastard as loud as she could shout. I told her not to set foot on my property again, and I'd rather die of thirst than walk inside Arturo's."

"She loves you, Señor Tom," Maria whispered. "She asks me about you every single day."

"I'd sooner keep a skunk under my bed than keep company with her!" he snapped, feeling his anger go on the rise. "She don't know a damn thing about lovin' a man. The only thing that whore loves is money! But she ain't gettin' no more of mine!"

The change in his voice convinced Maria to drop the subject. She went over to the door. "I will get your laundry," she said, then she disappeared inside.

Reminded of the tamales, he struggled out of his chair balancing the plate in one hand, fisting his whiskey in the other. He took a thirsty pull from the bottle. "Wish that damn whore would mind her own business, always askin' Maria about me. It ain't none of her affair in the first place, damn her."

The dog slipped past him on his way through the door, its nose aimed up at the plate of tamales. When he saw the dog in the house he yelled, "You damn sure ain't gettin' none of my supper, you worthless bastard. Go find yourself a rabbit. So help me, I'll let you starve before I feed you any of this.''

Moments later, as he was opening a second cornshuck wrapping around a delicious tamale, Maria hurried from the bedroom with an armload of clothes.

''Buenas noches,'' she said, letting herself out.

He waited until her footsteps faded to silence, then he looked down near his feet where the dog sat, watching him eat. ''If I had any poison, I'd feed it to you. Gunpowder is too damn expensive to waste on the likes of you.'' He took a bite off one end of the tamale, then he tossed the rest of it into the waiting jaws of his pet. ''Now get the hell away from me,'' he snarled. ''I hope that sets your worthless innards on fire. There ain't any water, and you're damn sure not gettin' any of this whiskey.''

Chapter Fourteen

He hadn't wanted to get drunk, not with such an important task facing him tomorrow. It had simply happened, and now he sat at his kitchen table with his surroundings out of focus, staring at an empty bottle in the dark. Cool night breezes lifted the curtains away from the windows now and then, though he hardly noticed. His thoughts were on the upcoming gunfight with Valdez . . . the draw he needed to make, his aim, and the bullet that would end the *pistolero's* life. He could see it all in his mind's eye. The slug would lift Valdez off his feet and slam him to the floor of a Guerrero saloon, or on the ground in the middle of the main street through town. It did not matter where the gunman died. His death was what counted, and Tom knew he could beat Valdez to the draw. He was sure of it.

"Time I went to bed," he mumbled thickly. His tongue refused to work properly when he said it. Steadying himself on the tabletop, he stood up slowly, his mind reeling atop a sea of whiskey. His side did not pain him at all now. The dog whimpered and scratched the door to be let outside before he went to bed. He took a staggering step in the dog's direction, then another, until he finally got up a head of steam that carried him on a weaving course to the front door. "Get out there and find where that goddamn chicken roosts," he said, the words mushy. "Kill the son of a bitch while he sleeps. That way you won't have to break a sweat, chasin' him all over the place. I'll hide the feathers in the morning' so Benito won't find 'em. There's a chicken dinner waitin' for you out there, you lazy bastard. All you gotta do is find it."

The dog trotted out on the porch, then it stopped and cocked its ears toward town. Tom had to close one eye to see the road clearly. Someone was walking slowly toward his house in the darkness, a figure he couldn't quite make out well enough to identify. "Maybe it's Maria," he said under his breath. Several times during the evening, he caught himself remembering the sight of her breasts as she bent down to kiss him.

He heard the dog whimper, and saw it wag its tail. Whoever was coming was a friend, someone the dog recognized. Tom held on to the door frame, closing one eye again, until he could see the figure well enough to know who it was.

"What the hell do you want?" he asked gruffly, feeling keen disappointment that it wasn't Maria.

Consuelo halted at the porch steps. For a time she said nothing at all.

"I asked you what the hell you're doin' here?" Tom said again. "You ain't welcome at my house no more."

He thought he heard sniffling, but he couldn't be sure.

"I came to say *adiós*," she finally replied.

He noticed that her voice was different somehow. *"Adiós?* I ain't leavin' town, if that's what you mean. I'm

156

stayin' 'til it rains, whenever that happens to be. The rest of 'em can all sell out, for all I care. But I'm stayin'. It'll rain this fall for sure.''

"That is not the reason," she said softly, sounding like she might be choking on something.

Another possibility entered his whiskey-fogged brain. "Does this mean that you're leavin' town? For good?" he asked, thinking about a triumphant return to the cantina after she was gone, perhaps with pretty Maria in her place.

"No," came the answer, and his hopes fell. "Maria told me that you are going after Luis Valdez tomorrow. I came to say goodbye."

At that moment, he could not guess why she cared. "It don't make much sense that you'd come. Last week, you said I was a bastard. Damn near every soul in Rio Blanco heard you say it, yellin' like you did."

"I was angry, Tom," she said in a pleading voice. "You say things to hurt me, and they make me angry."

A wave of dizziness forced him to tighten his grip on the door frame momentarily, which also gave him time to clear his thoughts. "I don't rightly remember what I said," he confessed. "Maybe in the mornin' I will."

Now he was sure Consuelo sniffled. "You tell me I am nothing but a whore," she said. "You say I am only interested in money. It is not true, Tom. I care . . . about other things."

"Like what?" he asked in a dull voice, as though he did not care.

She waited a considerable amount of time before she answered him. "I care about you, Tom. I thought we were . . . friends."

"We used to be," he replied, puzzled by the direction

157

the conversation was taking. He had fully expected more name-calling and screaming. "You started all this trouble between us, when you said I was gettin' too old to need a woman."

"You stopped coming to see me. For a month, you did not come at all."

"It's gotten too hot at night," he argued. "Don't seem it cools off at night like it used to. Besides, lately you've let yourself get fat. That's a part of the reason I quit comin' over." He looked at the soft bulges underneath her blouse and the widening of her hips. "If you'd look in the mirror every now and then, you'd know . . ."

She started to cry, tiny sobs that made her shoulders shake as she wiped the tears away with the back of her hand. "I am older, Tom, and so are you," she said in a tear-choked voice. "People change."

"I don't see that I've changed all that much," he protested. "Maybe I've got more gray hair than last year."

Consuelo regained her composure, dropping her hand to her side, no longer sobbing. "Perhaps only a little," she said softly.

He remembered what the doctor said about the care he'd been given during his recovery from the gunshot. According to Dr. Guthrie, he owed Consuelo his life. It would be better to thank her now, while he was drunk, he reasoned. The words would come a little easier. "I'm grateful for what you did for me, comin' every day to see to my wound. The soup was good, too. Doc Guthrie said I would have died without it, most likely. That medicine plant worked. Just wanted you to know I'm obliged."

"I only did it because I care for you," she whispered. "We were friends, but it is more than that. I . . . love

158

you, Tom. I have loved you for many years. These words are hard to say, because I know you do not have the same feelings for me. You think of me only as a *puta,* and it is something I can not change.''

He was growing more uncomfortable by the minute, listening to her describe her feelings. He wondered why she was telling him in the first place. ''I'm a shade too drunk tonight to talk about this,'' he began, clinging to the door frame with both hands when another wave of dizziness made things tilt. ''Maybe some other time, Consuelo, when I ain't quite so drunk.''

She nodded once. ''It is enough,'' she replied. ''I have said too much already. *Adiós,* Tom. May *Dios* be with you tomorrow when you face the *pistolero. Buenas noches.''*

She turned to leave, until his voice stopped her.

''I reckon we can still be friends,'' he said. ''I won't say nothin' else about how fat you've gotten if you won't say no more about me bein' too old to need a woman. It's this hot weather, and the dry spell, that takes my mind off urges.''

He was preparing to walk back inside, testing his legs for the trip to the bedroom, when he saw her climb the porch steps and come toward him. In the dark, he couldn't see her face to read her expression. She walked up to him and stood there, looking into his eyes.

''I will pray for your safe return,'' she said, then she traced a fingertip tenderly across his cheek. ''I love you, Tom. Even though you do not want the love of a *puta,* I will always love you, no matter what you say to me.''

''I wish you wouldn't talk like that,'' he muttered, attempting to stand unassisted on unsteady legs. ''I hardly know what to say when you're bein' nice.''

Very quickly, before he could object, she stood on her tiptoes and planted a kiss on his mouth. She was whirling away when he realized what she'd done, but she was already starting down the porch steps before he could reach for her.

He stood near the door until she went out of sight behind the cantina. Swaying this way and that, he closed the door with a bang and stumbled through the darkness to his bed.

"You look half dead this mornin'," Jessie said, watching Tom struggle into his boots. "Your eyeballs look like they were fried, Tom. What the hell did you do to yourself last night?"

His head was splitting and the last thing he wanted was a question. It hurt to talk, or move. Just sitting on the edge of the mattress was like having a wedge driven into his skull. The only consolation was that his side didn't pain him. "I got drunk," he answered feebly, working his foot into the second boot, grimacing. "Didn't plan to. It just worked out that way."

"I've seen corpses that looked better," Jessie remarked, showing off his toothless grin. "I stopped by to see if you had a hankerin' to ride down for another look at your cattle. That sucking mud oughta be checked every day for bogged cows. But you damn sure don't look like a man who can sit a saddle this mornin', so I suppose I'll go by myself."

"I can ride," Tom growled. "I'm ridin' down to Guerrero tonight. Gonna have that little set-to with Luis Valdez."

Jessie's grin vanished. "I'll go fetch my six-shooter,"

he said solemnly. "Cleaned it an' oiled it the other day. We can check on the cattle on our way down."

"No need for you to go, Jess," he said, resting after putting on the last boot. His skull was swimming and he felt nauseous. Something like cotton coated his tongue. "I can handle this alone."

"I'm goin'," Jessie replied. "There were three of them. Don't play the part of a bull-headed fool. You need all the help you can get against those odds."

Gradually, the room ceased its spin. Tom pushed up from the bed and took a tentative step toward the bedroom door. He groaned when his weight shifted. It was as if someone had dropped an anvil on top of his head. "I need a drink," he said hoarsely, like he had pebbles in his throat. "Clear out of my way, Jess. I'm liable to fall down any second."

Jessie backed into the front room, watching Tom take tiny, mincing steps on the balls of his feet toward the table where the cases of whiskey sat. "Maybe today wouldn't be such a good day to go lookin' fer a gunfight, Tom," he offered. "You don't look so good just now."

"I'll heal before sundown," Tom croaked, arriving at the table just as his strength and balance both played out. Pressing a palm to the tabletop, he reached into the open crate and withdrew a fresh bottle, giving only a passing glance to the empty jug in front of a chair. He pulled the cork with his teeth and let it fall to the floor, fearing the risks of using the hand supporting him. The scent of barley vapors assailed his nose as he took a healthy swallow. His eyes closed while the liquid scalded his throat.

"Damn," he hissed when he could catch his breath. "A snakebite can't feel no worse'n this." He eased his weight down in the chair and took a deep breath. "I'd sooner be drug to death by a wild horse than have a hangover."

"You ain't got any color in your face," Jessie observed. "All the blood's run to your eyes. I wouldn't touch no more of that stuff if I was you. You look sicker'n a foundered mule."

Tom drank again, not from defiance, simply need. His hands were shaking violently and it felt like his skull would burst. "If I want your advice, I'll ask for it," he grumbled. "This is the only cure there is."

Jessie approached the table cautiously, made wary by Tom's mood. "A man who's gonna look death in the eye hadn't oughta do it with a bellyful of whiskey. You'll need to be fast, Tom. And clearheaded to boot. Put the cork back in that jug. I'm askin' as a friend."

The cork lay on the floor near Tom's boots. He stared at it for a while. "I know you're right, Jess, but there's a cannonball rollin' around inside my head. I need to steady my nerves."

"Just so they don't get too steady," Jessie said. "This is liable to be the most dangerous gunfight you was ever in."

As Tom's head started to clear, he wondered if Jessie could be right. Would Luis Valdez be the fastest gunman he had ever faced? Faster than Bill Allison? Faster than Buck Ramsey in the prime of his gunfighting career? Tom had bested them all, but was Valdez a fraction faster than any of the others? The warning from Ranger Captain Trav Hollaman echoed through his mind. "I'm faster," he told Jessie, but without the same conviction he felt before. Doubts began creeping into his thoughts.

162

He took a long, bubbling swallow of whiskey, wondering.

"When were you aimin' to leave?" Jessie asked, watching Tom's hands shake.

"Middle of the afternoon, Jess," he replied. "I'd be obliged if you'd drop by to saddle my horse. I can't quite manage swingin' that saddle over the bay's back just yet."

Jessie turned away from the table. "I'll be here around three," he said. "I'll be wearin' a gun."

Jessie clumped over to the door and let himself out. For a moment Tom sat, listening to a faint ringing in his ears, until he heard Jessie's horse swing away from the porch. Then he directed his attention to the empty bottle across the table. "I'll practice my aim one more time," he said, "soon as my hands get steady."

He drank again and got up to strap on his gunbelt, tying the holster down to his right leg. The throbbing headache which had awakened him this morning lessened. He took the empty bottle and walked slowly out on the porch, squinting when bright sunlight hurt his eyes.

Moving down the steps gingerly so as not to jiggle his brain, he started toward the stump in a careful walk. The whiskey he drank moments before started to help. By the time he arrived at the stump he felt better. He placed the bottle just so and began measuring the paces. Once, he touched his side and was pleased to discover that he felt no pain.

Thirty paces from the stump, he turned around slowly. His right hand moved close to the gun, poised, fingers curling. Sighting the reflected glare from the bottle, he went into his crouch and tensed the muscles in his arm.

"Adiós, you thievin' bastard," he whispered to the imaginary Valdez. "You just bought yourself a plot of ground on Boot Hill."

He set his arm in motion, down to the gun butt, then upward in a lightning-fast arc. The Colt roared, slamming into his palm with a kick he felt all the way to his shoulder. Exploding glass showered to the ground around the stump, catching the sun's rays briefly in midflight. When the last tiny fragments fluttered to earth, Tom lowered the muzzle of the .44 and gave a grunt of satisfaction.

He heard Delia's back door open before he put the gun away.

"Goodness me!" the woman exclaimed. "I wish you'd warn a body beforehand, Tom. I was just lying down for my nap. You gave me an awful fright."

If he told the truth he would have said that he enjoyed envisioning what it must have looked like when a gunshot jolted Delia from her daybed. Instead, he turned to her and holstered his gun. "Sorry about the disturbance, Miz Cummings. This'll be the last time I practice so early in the morning. I'm gonna kill a man tonight over in Mexico, the one who's been stealin' our cattle. Just wanted to be sure of my aim."

Delia clapped a hand over her mouth, though Tom knew it wouldn't stay there long. "There are times when you can be most disgusting," she said, lowering her hand, raising her head so she looked down her nose at him. "I'm thoroughly revolted, Tom Culpepper, to learn that I've been living beside a cold-blooded murderer all these years. My Clarence insisted that you had changed. If he were alive today, he'd know just how wrong he was about you! A leopard never loses its spots."

He started back to the house without saying any more to Delia, knowing it was a waste of time. Benito's wife and children had come out to see who was doing the shooting. He merely nodded politely and walked to his porch steps. A good feeling bolstered his spirits after the perfect shot at the bottle and he'd be damned if he would allow Delia or anybody else to spoil it.

Chapter Fifteen

As they swung their horses away from the corral fence, Tom saw the crowd gathered at the cantina. For some reason, he hadn't noticed it before. More than a dozen residents of Rio Blanco stood in the shade of the cantina porch to watch Tom and Jessie ride out. He was touched by their show of interest, even Chap Grant's, who stood by himself near the cantina door. For the moment, Chap's cowardice was forgotten as Tom gave everyone a lazy wave.

"Folks came to town to see you off, Tom," Jessie remarked, his face turned to the crowd. "Yonder's the Wardlaw boys. Chap, too. Everybody was talkin' about it down at the *mercado* when I went in to get a plug of tobacco."

From the corner of his eye, Tom caught a glimpse of Consuelo at one end of the porch. She was wearing a yellow skirt and a white blouse with a plunging neckline. Just then, she did not look as fat as he remembered. "Must be that dress," he muttered, looking straight ahead so no one would notice that he saw Consuelo. They headed their horses south, riding past the

cantina at a distance. Tom knew everyone was watching
. . . he didn't need a second look.

Leaving Rio Blanco behind, Tom pulled his hat brim
over his eyes to keep out a late-day sun. For reasons he
couldn't explain, there was no wind today, not so much
as a breath of air from any direction. A boiling cloud of
caliche dust arose behind their horses, hanging in the
stillness, swirling and curling about before settling
slowly back to earth like powdery snow. Tom kept his
eyes on the horizon, his mouth set in a grim line. Beyond the tops of the brush stretching before them, just
across the Rio Grande, he had an appointment with the
fates. A duel was about to be fought, and in the end,
one man would live. The other would die.

They came to the banks of the Rio Grande at dusk.
To the west, a setting sun emblazoned the sky with its
hues of red and purple. A thin line of low clouds held
false promise far to the west. Tom knew they offered no
chances of rain. Halting their horses on a low bluff above
the river, they sat in silence for a time. Tom stared at
the sluggish current moving past them toward the distant
gulf, but his mind had already made the crossing ahead
of him to the dusty little Mexican village of Guerrero.
He knew Luis Valdez would be there in one of the cantinas, and Tom was just as certain that in a few hours
more, blood would be spilled on the cantina floor.

"Glad there wasn't any cows balled up in that mud,"
Jessie said. It was an effort to talk about most anything
else. Tom had fallen into a moody silence as soon as
they left Rio Blanco. Hardly a word was said all the way
to the Mexican border.

"Let's get across, Jess," Tom said quietly. He touched the bay with a spur and started down the embankment.

Jessie hurried his chestnut and fell in beside Tom before the horses splashed into the river's shallows. The bay snorted once when it felt uncertain footing. Tom let the horse have its head. The gelding was seasoned to the river and it would avoid the treacherous quicksand beds. Jessie kept his right hand on the butt of his Mason Colt while his horse navigated the river. Tom found some amusement when Jessie arrived wearing the gun. The old pistol was rusted by years of neglect, despite Jessie's attempt to oil it. In truth, there had been no need for a gun around Rio Blanco for quite a spell, unless you counted killing snakes or an occasional coyote. But all that had changed suddenly, with the return of Luis Valdez to his old border haunts. In many respects, Tom was glad to have the chance to demonstrate his skill with a gun in spite of the danger. The past few years, he'd begun to feel useless, out of step with the times, as if nobody cared about his comings and goings. It was good to be the center of attention again, to feel the stares others gave him.

In the deepest spots, the river never touched the bellies of the horses. The bay struck a trot as soon as it reached the far bank, and the jolt of its gait awakened the pain in Tom's side. He winced and slowed the gelding to a walk. He'd almost forgotten about the bullet hole until now. Reaching back to one of Hank's borrowed saddlebags, he took out the bottle of whiskey. "My damn side hurts," he said, to the question in Jessie's eyes. Withdrawing the cork with his teeth, he offered the bottle to Jessie first. The old cowboy shook his head.

"I'm stayin' sober," he replied. "Can't hardly shoot straight unless I am."

Tom downed a generous swallow, then another. Half the contents of the bottle was missing when he replaced the cork. The horses climbed the opposite bank, to the dim ruts of a seldom used wagon road leading to Guerrero. The sky darkened above them, permitting the first stars of night to show off their brilliance.

"When we get to town," Tom began, "I want you to stay out of sight. We'll find an alley someplace where you can keep the horses. I aim to be on solid ground when I challenge Valdez this time."

"I said I'd go with you," Jessie argued. "Somebody's got to back your move, so them other *pistoleros* don't jump in. We can tie these horses in the alley, but I'm goin' with you to the cantinas to watch your backside."

"This isn't your fight," he said, hoping to end it there.

Jessie seemed to be in deep thought. "It's any feller's fight when the odds stack up wrong," he offered later.

Tom let the matter drop. Following the snakelike course of the wagon road running beside the river, they rode side by side in silence. Off in the brush, night birds called. Farther away, an owl hooted once, then twice more. Guided by faint starlight, they entered a group of low hills. A mile farther on lay the village. Soon they would be able to see the lights from the cantina windows. Tom started to notice a knot forming in his belly. Had Jessie not been there, he would have taken another drink just then.

"Yonder it is," Jessie remarked, as they crossed the top of a brush-choked hill.

Guerrero sat in a shallow basin. Adobe huts were scattered around the business district, lanterns and can-dles illuminating windows across town. On both sides of a single street running north to south, larger buildings were crowded together, the stores and shops of Guerrero, and its cantinas. Pale caliche made the road appear to glow beneath the night sky filled with stars, in stark contrast to the darker shapes of the adobes. On the south side of town, a church steeple towered above the low rooftops. Tom remembered that Guerrero was one of the oldest *pueblos* in the north of Mexico, once a headquarters for the efforts by Franciscan priests to Christianize Indian tribes in the region, the savage Yaqui, the Lipan Apaches, and the southernmost Comanche bands.

Their horses started down a gentle grade that would take them to the outskirts of town. Now Tom wanted a drink more than ever, as a tiny tremor began in his fingertips. To keep his hands busy, he drew his Colt and thumbed open the loading gate to check the shells in the cylinder. He had loaded it carefully around noon, making a second look unnecessary. But when he dropped the gun back in his holster, he felt better. The tremors had ceased, for now.

Near the first adobe dwellings, they could hear faint music coming from the center of town. A guitar played a lilting melody to the accompaniment of a harmonica. As they entered the north end of Guerrero to ride down its main street, Tom pulled the bay to a halt and frowned.

"Let's swing off an' ride behind those stores," he said, pointing to a spot behind the buildings on the west side of the road. "Keep your eyes open for that white stud. Valdez won't be far away."

They reined off the road, to pick their way among the huts and small livestock sheds. A dog barked near one of the houses when it heard the approaching horses. A

171

light sweat had begun to form on Tom's skin, dampening his palms. He rubbed them dry on his pants, mildly annoyed.

A large cantina loomed in front of them. Golden light spilled from its rear windows, and from the open doorway of a kitchen off the back. Music and laughter, and the hum of conversation, came from the building. In the bad light, Tom could barely see places where adobe mud had peeled away from the walls.

He signaled a stop beside the gnarled trunk of a mesquite tree. The dog had stopped barking, and now there were only the sounds from the cantina. "We'll leave our horses here while we take a look at the hitch rail around front," he said in a low voice, swinging his right foot over the rump of the bay to dismount.

Jessie was tying the chestnut's reins to a limb before Tom reached the ground. Without taking his eyes from the cantina windows, Tom looped his reins around the limb and then started for a dark passageway between the cantina and a smaller building with blackened panes of glass. He heard Jessie plodding along behind him. Unconsciously, Tom's right hand went to the butt of his .44.

He came to a brightly lit cantina window and halted to peer inside, standing at the edge of the shadow so he wouldn't be seen. Spread across an uneven dirt floor, rough-cut plank tables held an assortment of drinkers and card players. *Cigarillo* smoke hung in filmy layers across the room, thickening near the ceiling where lantern globes shed light on the cantina's activities. The smoke did not hide the smell of unwashed bodies emanating from the window, or the stale scent of pulque clinging to empty mugs at the tables. Tom could hear bits and pieces of conversations here and there above the soft strumming of a guitar and the wheeze of a badly played harmonica coming from a spot near the back wall. Tom let his gaze drift across the faces at the tables, seeking the one he would recognize. Now and then a gale of laughter would erupt at a gathering of drinkers, the sudden noise attracting his attention until he was certain Valdez was not among them. Slowly, he examined every face in the crowd.

"Valdez ain't here," he whispered to Jessie. "Let's have a look across the street."

They made their way soundlessly down the passageway to the road, where Tom signaled a halt to look at the hitch rails for the white Spanish stud. Row upon row of resting, hipshot horses and mules stood on either side of the street, but there was no white animal among them anywhere.

"Maybe he keeps the stud at a livery," Tom said quietly. "That will be the next place we look." He remembered a stable on the east side of the village, a ramshackle barn and crude corrals fashioned from crooked mesquite limbs. "Don't let any grass grow under your feet gettin' across this road," he added over his shoulder. "Don't want anybody to know we're here until I'm ready."

He started across the empty street, worrying that the white stud might be back at the canyon where he found the horse and the stolen cattle the first time. It was an important part of his plan to take back the horse, if he could, but only after Valdez was dead would he direct his attention to recovering the stud. He crept to the darkness of another alleyway between a *mercado* and a slant-roofed vegetable market. Silhouetted against the night sky, he could see the top of the livery barn just to the east of the road.

As they left the rear of the *mercado,* something caught Tom's eye behind a building farther to the south. Standing in a square of lantern light from a back door of a noisy cantina, the white stallion had its head lowered with a saddle tied to its withers . . . it was Tom's saddle, for he recognized it at once. He halted in midstride and squared around. "There's the stud," he said, as anger hardened his cheeks. "Valdez will be inside." He took a deep breath and looked at Jessie. "If you're still hankerin' to lend me a hand, stay close to that back door. If Valdez's *compadres* are inclined to stick their noses into this affair, I'll yell for you to come inside. Come with that gun drawn, Jess. There won't be much time to claw for leather."

Jessie pulled his Colt and nodded. "I'll be ready, Tom," he replied, showing his empty gums in a humorless grin. "Best you duck down when I come through that back door, 'cause I'll be throwin' lead all over the place."

He clapped the old man on the shoulder. "You're a good friend, Jess," he said softly. "Damn near everybody else in Rio Blanco ran short of nerve when it came time to stand up and be counted. I owe you."

He started around to the front of the cantina, until an afterthought made him pause. "If anything happens to me, clear out of town as fast as you can travel, so you can make the river ahead of Valdez and his boys. If Valdez is faster, don't hang around to see how it ends. I'd ask that you feed that ol' spotted dog of mine. Hell, you can keep him, along with the cows I've got left. Got no family to leave 'em to anyway. The dog's worth even less than my cows, so I ain't leavin' you much. See that Consuelo gets the house and what furniture I've got. It's mostly junk. I keep some money under my mattress. You can split it with Consuelo. I owe her, too. She saved my life after I took that slug. I reckon the two of you are the only friends I've got.''

''Don't talk like that, Tom,'' Jessie protested, trying to keep his voice low. ''You're startin' to sound like a feller who's already diggin' his own grave.''

He hesitated a moment longer, trying to think of a way to explain. If he could, he wanted to preserve his dignity. ''It was mostly on account of the dog, just in case somethin' goes wrong tonight. A man's luck can turn bad . . .'' He turned and walked into the alley, wishing he hadn't said quite so much.

Rounding the corner, he went past three darkened buildings to the front of the cantina with his heart laboring mightily inside his chest. Passing a window, he glanced inside without slowing his footsteps. There were only a few patrons at the tables. Three men stood in front of a makeshift bar, upended flour kegs supporting wooden planks and an assortment of mugs, glasses, and bottles. Light from the open door loomed across his path as he continued along the front of the building, a square of yellow where he would make the turn to go inside. His heart was hammering now, as he came abreast of the doorway. He saw a slender Mexican youth leaning against the outer wall, partly hidden in the shadows. He ignored the boy and turned into the cantina, his right hand poised near his gun.

Less than a dozen drinkers occupied the tables. Most wore the white cotton homespun common to Mexican goat herders. A couple of *vaqueros* idled at the bar, but

175

Tom merely glanced at them, for his attention was drawn to a corner table where the lantern light was poor. Seated with his back to the wall, Luis Valdez looked up when Tom entered the room. Once again, he was flanked by the two *pistoleros* who had ridden with him to Rio Blanco.

Tom squared himself, facing Valdez. The drone of conversation stopped. Heads turned, and suddenly there was an eerie silence in the place.

"You!" Tom snarled, spreading his feet slightly apart, aiming the index finger of his left hand at Valdez. "Stand up real slow! You an' me have got a score to settle!"

Valdez tilted his head back, allowing Tom a glimpse of his face below the broad brim of his sombrero. A thick black beard parted to show his teeth as the gunman smiled. His hands rested on the tabletop in front of him. He kept them there, rock-still, as if he had all the time in the world. "You have come back from the dead," he said in broken English, each word pronounced slowly in a gravelly voice. "Perhaps you are like *el gato?* A cat with many lives?"

Tom lowered his hand. Every muscle in his body was tensed for the moment when Valdez called for the draw. "You should have killed me when you had the chance," he said evenly, hardly noticing anyone else in the room, his gaze fixed on Valdez's hands. "Get up from that table, Luis. I'm gonna give you one more chance to fill your hand."

The gunman simply shrugged at first, still wearing his leering grin. "I will kill you this time, *Tejano,*" he said quietly. *"En la mañana,* I will feed your carcass to the dogs of Guerrero."

Tom managed his own one-sided grin. "We'll see. Stand up and go for your gun."

Valdez glanced left, then right, to the faces of the men on either side of him, then he drew his feet under him and started slowly out of the chair.

Chapter Sixteen

Two *vaqueros* at a neighboring table raised their hands to show them empty, then they slid out of their chairs and crept away toward the bar to be out of the line of fire. Tom watched Valdez rise to his feet, and now the lantern light caught streaks of gray in his beard and the shoulder-length hair below the crown of his sombrero. Light glinted off the brass-jacketed cartridges in the twin belts across his thick chest, though Tom gave the belts and the gunman's face only passing notice. His attention was directed to the pair of pistols at the Mexican's sides. When either hand made a move toward one of the guns, he would draw.

"Pendejo!" Valdez spat, as his curled fingertips inched slightly closer to his pistol grips.

The insult was a trick, as old as the gunfighter's profession, to make Tom angry. To distract him. "We'll see who's the fool," he replied matter-of-factly.

Valdez spoke to his companions. *"Vamos,"* he hissed, without taking his eyes off Tom.

The two *pistoleros* stood up cautiously. Tom feared it might be another trick to draw notice away from Valdez's hands, but he was forced to ignore the other gunmen. Valdez posted the greatest danger.

"You'll be the first to die if either one of 'em goes for his gun," Tom warned, crouching, curling his fingers.

Valdez laughed. "They are only boys," he said. "Let this be between us, *Tejano*. Let us fight like men."

Both *pistoleros* backed slowly away from the table. Someone coughed at the back of the room, then there was silence again. Tom could hear the gentle hiss of the coal oil lanterns, and the hammering beat of his own heart.

"Any time," Tom offered, speaking just above a whisper. "I'm givin' you the first move, same as I gave all the others. You're a dead man, Luis. All you gotta do is make the draw."

The muscles in Valdez's shoulders bunched slightly . . . Tom saw it beneath the fabric of his shirt. He's ready now, Tom thought. All the palaver is over.

Scenes from Tom's past flashed through his memory, of other gunfights, other faces staring at him in the final seconds before a duel began. Bill Allison's confident expression. Buck Ramsey's arrogant challenge moments before pistols were drawn. Time was measured in fractions of a second as the deadly contests opened. Once again, in the steamy heat of this Guerrero cantina, Tom was gambling that his reflexes would be a fraction faster.

He sensed that Valdez was waiting for something, as the seconds ticked away in the soundless room. Vowing that he wouldn't allow himself to be tricked into glancing in another direction, he forced his eyes to remain on the Mexican's hands. He knew he could beat Valdez to the draw easily if he pulled first. But it was a point of honor, something his conscience demanded, to allow the *pistolero* to drop either hand before he clawed leather.

Suddenly, he heard the quiet, cautious placement of a foot behind him . . . the soft sound was very close. Someone approached him from the rear.

"You said we'd settle this like men," he growled. "Tell the back-shooter behind me to back off . . ."

He couldn't risk looking behind him, not with Valdez poised for a draw. Another footfall broke the silence.

"You yellow bastard!" Tom snarled. "Call off your back-shooter!"

The whisper of moving air was his only warning. Something struck the back of his head and he went reeling forward, staggering, trying to keep his balance. A field of flashing lights appeared before his eyes. The toe of his boot caught and he went sprawling on his chest, tasting dirt. A burst of laughter echoed back and forth across the room as he slipped toward unconsciousness. He tried to push himself up from the floor . . . his arms were like lead weights . . . he couldn't move them.

His vision blurred. Off in the distance, he heard a muffled gunshot, but there was no pain. Then his eyes batted shut and he felt nothing.

Dim lights pierced the darkness, then evaporated, and his world turned black again. Slowly, his surroundings grayed like a sky just before dawn. He heard himself groan . . . it was as if the sound came from the bottom of a well.

When his eyes opened fully, he saw a roof of adobe mud. "Where am I?" he wondered aloud. He let his gaze roam to either side, until he saw a wall of iron bars. "What the hell am I doin' in jail?" he asked.

He managed to get one elbow underneath him despite a numbness in his limbs, rolling shakily to one side for a better view of the bars. Blinking, waiting for his eyes to focus properly, he examined the tiny cell where he found himself. He was lying on a cot in a room surrounded on three sides by rusty iron bars, roughly a ten-foot square with a low roof that would barely allow him to stand. The adobe wall behind him had no window. Shafts of sunlight beamed into the building from a barred door at the end of a three-foot hallway. Gradually, he became aware of the heat. His clothing was plastered to his skin. When he took a deep breath, the stench of urine was overpowering. Two more cells, one on either side of his, were empty.

He sat up and swung his legs off the cot. He'd been resting on a lumpy mattress stuffed with cornshucks. Before his feet reached the floor he noticed a dull pain at the back of his skull. He touched the spot with a fingertip, finding a knot beneath matted strands of hair. The bump reminded him of the blow he was given from behind as he waited for Valdez to go for his guns. "Somebody cold-cocked me," he mumbled. "This must be the Guerrero jail."

He remembered sensing that Valdez was waiting for something, a hesitation, perhaps a slight flicker of recognition in the *pistolero's* eyes. He'd known something was wrong, but unwilling to chance taking a look behind him that might give Valdez the advantage, he'd simply stood his ground until the blow came. "I heard a gun go off someplace," he remembered. Then the cold realization struck him, that the shot might have been meant for Jessie Kootz in the alley behind the cantina.

He buried his face in his hands, resting his elbows on his knees. If anything had happened to Jessie, he could never forgive himself for allowing the old man to ride into a fight he had no part of. The other jail cells were empty. Had Jessie gotten away?

"Damn," he muttered. He wouldn't allow himself to think about a worse fate for Jessie. Not now. Not until he knew for sure. He got up slowly and walked to his cell door, ducking down so the top of his head would miss the low roof. Wrapping both hands around the bars, he tested the lock with a nudge. Heavy iron rattled, answering his question. They had remembered to lock him inside.

An unwanted recollection entered his thoughts, of Chap Grant's warning that they might rot away in a Mexican jail the rest of their lives if they crossed over to go after the stolen cows. Was this to be Tom Culpepper's fate? To die of old age in a Guerrero cell? Or of dysentery from spoiled food and bad water?

Such gloomy prospects had to be considered, he knew. Mexican jails were notorious for bad treatment of prisoners. He let out a sigh and turned away from the bars. The revenge he sought against Luis Valdez had ended in disastrous failure. He wondered who had delivered the blow to the back of his head. The two gunmen who rode with Valdez were standing in plain sight when someone hit him. There had only been the skinny boy outside.

He sank to the cot in a black mood. Of late, it seemed almost everything had gone awry. Was it just bad luck that all his fortunes took a downturn?

He found he couldn't keep his mind off Jessie. The

old cowboy would have been no match for Valdez or any of his shooters. That lone gunshot refused to leave Tom's memory. The sound had come from far away, perhaps from the alley where Jessie was waiting for Tom's signal to rush through the rear door.

"It wasn't his fight," he told himself sadly, resting his chin in the palm of a hand. "I shouldn't have let him come, damn it! I should have told him to stay out of my affairs."

In the midst of his dark ruminations, he heard sounds outside. The unmistakable rattle of a cart, wheels grinding and creaking over hard ground, passed near the jail. The noises faded, until he was again surrounded by the absolute silence of his cell.

"I'll go loco in here," he predicted, measuring the size of his iron cage with his eyes. "In a couple of months I'll be screamin' my head off." He'd never been the kind who could tolerate tight places very long. Even his house became too small at times, forcing him out into the heat when he couldn't stand the confinement any longer.

Despair closed in on him. His fate was as predictable as the next sunrise. He would slowly succumb to madness in this jail cell, if dysentery did not claim him first. No one would know about his suffering except his captors, and they would enjoy it, when T.C. Culpepper lost his mind, or wasted away to a skeleton like the cattle around Rio Blanco.

Later, he rested his head against the adobe wall, closing his eyes. The heat in the small building became unbearable. Sweat rolled off his forehead, down his cheeks. His shirt clung to him like a second skin. As the temperature increased, so did the urine smell in his cell. "I can't take many days of this,'' he said aloud, as much to hear the sound of his voice as the need to complain. The silence in the jail only worsened his irritation over being confined. He began to fear the silence in the same way he feared imprisonment. One or the other would soon drive him mad.

He tried not to think about Jessie. The burden of the old man's death, the knowledge that Jessie might have died trying to help him, was too painful to think about. Thus he made up his mind that until he knew otherwise, he would force himself to believe that Jessie had escaped.

The square of striped sunlight coming from the barred window in the front door of the jail moved slowly across the dirt floor, marking the passage of time. No matter how hard Tom listened, there was no sound outside the jail. He guessed the building was some distance from the center of Guerrero, explaining the silence. Other than the passing of that single cart earlier in the day, no one had come close enough for him to hear them.

Gradually, the sky beyond the window paled with sunset. Even more slowly, the air in the jail cooled. He got up to pace back and forth across his cell when the temperature allowed it, keeping his head bowed to avoid bumping the roof. He could manage just three short strides before he came to the bars and turned around. ''It's too goddamn small,'' he muttered bitterly.

The sounds of footsteps halted his pacing. He turned to watch the door. A key was used on the lock. Tom gripped the bars, preparing himself for his first look at whoever held him prisoner.

A paunchy man in a deep blue tunic entered the jail. His uniform was trimmed in scarlet, marking him as a

Federale. Shoulder boards announced the fact that he held the rank of colonel. When Tom saw the colonel's face, fleshy jaws, and a pencil mustache, he knew he could count on a healthy dose of misery. The man had close-set eyes, hooded by drooping lids, and by the way he carried himself down the hallway in front of the cells, the colonel had a high opinion of himself and his importance. Following close behind, a slack-jawed soldier with a corporal's stripes on the arms of his tunic carried a rusty tin plate and a spoon. Above the stench of urine, Tom caught a whiff of something rancid, no doubt the supper the corporal brought him.

The colonel stopped in front of Tom's cell. He was much shorter than Tom and had to look up to meet his gaze. *"Buenas tardes,* Señor Culpepper," he said. Tom could see the hatred in his eyes.

"Why am I being jailed?" Tom asked.

The colonel glanced down at his polished boots, then back to Tom before he answered. "I am Colonel Ortega," he began, *"Comandante* of the garrison of Guerrero. You are in my jail for a host of charges. Theft of cattle. Stealing a horse. Threatening the life of a good citizen of this *pueblo.* Shall I continue?"

Tom's hands tightened around the bars. "Those were my cows in the first place. I got them back, after Valdez stole them from us! Same goes for that white stud . . . he was stolen, too, an' I offered Valdez the chance to go for his gun first, until somebody swatted me on the head while my back was turned!"

The corporal carrying Tom's food gave a lopsided grin. "I was the one who hit you, señor," he said, with a sideways glance to Ortega after he said it.

"I demand you release me!" Tom cried, his arms

trembling with building rage. "I've committed no crime in Mexico, and you know damn well I'm tellin' the truth!"

Ortega smiled. "You demand this of me?" he asked, as though he enjoyed a joke. Then he threw back his head and laughed. "You . . . are making a demand?" he roared, then his laughter stopped.

The corporal chuckled. *"Idiota,"* he said. "You can make no demand in Guerrero! This is not Texas!"

"Let me out of here," Tom growled, pressing his face close to the bars. "You know damn well those were my cows."

Ortega's grin disappeared, and now his eyelids drooped more than ever. "You will be a guest here for a very long time, Señor Culpepper, unless the heat or the scorpions kill you first. You are my prisoner. I will decide how long you stay. For the crimes you are charged with, I can keep you here for twenty . . . perhaps thirty years." He glanced at the dish in the corporal's hands. "Corporal Ramirez has your supper. You will be fed *frijoles* once a day. A cup of water is given in the morning. Do not waste anything, señor, or the ration will be cut in half. Do not attempt to escape. No one has ever escaped from the Guerrero jail." Now his eyes seemed to bore through Tom. "If you try something foolish, my corporal has orders to kill you."

Corporal Ramirez removed a ring of keys from an inside pocket of his tunic. He opened the lock to Tom's cell and then placed the plate of beans on the floor while Ortega rested his hand on the butt of his pistol. When the door was locked, Ortega gave a satisfied grunt and wheeled away from the cell with the corporal close at his heels.

Tom ignored the food for the moment . . . he had to know what had happened to Jessie. "What about the old man who came with me?" he asked.

Ortega stopped midway to the jail door and looked over his shoulder. "Unfortunately, your friend rode back to Texas before we could place him under arrest. However, if he crosses the border again he will be executed. He shot one of my men behind the cantina last night. We chased him to the river, but he was riding a good horse and we could not catch him. Miguel will die from his wound and then your *compadre* will be wanted for murder."

A feeling of relief loosened the knot in Tom's belly. Jessie had made his escape. As though a tremendous weight had been lifted from his shoulders, he turned his attention to the plate of beans on the floor of his cell.

Chapter Seventeen

The monotony was edging him closer to madness. Days passed, each one the same as the day before. By the middle of the afternoon, the heat inside the jail became so oppressive that he had trouble breathing. He paced back and forth until he was exhausted, until the heat drained him. Only at night was there any escape. Corporal Ramirez came every morning with a cup of water, which he passed between the bars. Just before sundown, he came with a plate of watery beans smelling suspiciously of offal. When Tom ate a few of the beans to sustain his failing strength, a bellyache followed in a few hours. By the fifth day of his imprisonment, the recurring bouts of dysentery had weakened him so that he stopped pacing altogether.

When he slept, his dreams were frightening things. He often dreamed of being locked in a dark closet, unable to move, suffocating on stale air. In his dream, he banged on the door and cried for help until he couldn't breathe. Then he would awaken with a start and sit up on the cot, gasping for air. Day by day, he knew he was slowly losing his mind. More and more, he carried on conversations with himself to end the monotonous silence. And as the cramps in his abdomen worsened after each meal, he started to wonder if the poisoned food would eventually kill him. The small hole in the floor of his cell where he relieved himself gave off such terrible odors that Corporal Ramirez wore a bandana over his nose when he brought the food and water.

Darkness finally settled over the land, cooling the air inside the jail. Tom sat on the edge of his bunk, lost in the depths of his despair, until he heard the braying of a jackass in the distance. He raised his head to listen closely. Had it not been for the reality of the bars around him, he could have imagined that it was Pedro's jackass begging for food, for the braying was exactly the same. He knew, of course, that it wasn't Pedro's animal. The sound reminded him of Pedro's pretty daughter and he conjured up memories of Maria, to pass the time. Later, when the cramps grew less, he rested his head against the adobe wall to doze.

A sound startled him. He heard voices close to the jail, and when he looked to the window at the top of the door into the building, he saw lantern light flickering beyond the bars. A woman laughed, a girlish giggle, while footsteps came closer and the light grew brighter.

"Mas tequila?" the woman asked. Tom could have sworn he knew the voice.

"Como no?" a man's voice replied, the voice of Corporal Ramirez.

Tom heard the soft pop of a cork, then bubbling noises as the corporal swallowed.

"Gracias, mi hija," Ramirez said breathlessly.

"De nada, muy guapo soldado," the woman replied.

Tom recognized the voice at once. He couldn't believe his ears. What was Consuelo doing here? Why was she giving tequila to Corporal Ramirez? Telling him he was a handsome soldier? Tom was bewildered by Consuelo's presence in Guerrero. Why had she come to the jail?

Consuelo giggled, then she whispered something Tom couldn't hear. Moments later, the lantern was extinguished, then the cork popped again very close to the door.

Minutes passed. Tom heard the soft sounds of scraping feet and every now and then, a contented sigh. Tom got up quietly and crept to the door of his cell, cocking an ear. He allowed himself to consider the possibility that Consuelo had come to Guerrero to try to help him break out of jail. It was the only explanation for her presence. Or was it only wishful thinking on his part? Thinking about the chances of escape, his heart began to pound.

"Estoy muy borracho," he heard the corporal say, telling Consuelo that he was drunk.

Consuelo murmured something. Ramirez laughed. More swallowing sounds filtered through the barred window, bringing a smile to Tom's face. Consuelo was getting the corporal drunk. If her plan worked, she would have no problem taking the corporal's keys.

Tom thought about the distance they had to travel to reach the border. Without a horse, could they make it before his escape was discovered? How had Consuelo gotten there? For a moment, all he could think about were loose ends. He didn't have a gun. Ramirez carried a pistol. If Consuelo got the jail unlocked, he could take the corporal's gun, giving them a fighting chance to make the river if pursuit caught up too quickly. Tom knew his weakened condition would keep him from walking all the way to the border. He had to find a horse, even though it would add to the risk of discovery when he stole one from Guerrero. A barking dog, or a watchful neighbor, could send up an alarm.

He thought about Consuelo, the courage she was showing to come to rescue him. He'd been wrong to accuse her of thinking only of money. She was risking her life for him now. Holding on to the bars, he stood in the darkness, wondering why she felt any loyalty to him after all the harsh words he'd spoken to her.

Shattering glass abruptly ended the stillness outside the jail. Someone groaned . . . it was a man's voice. Then he heard the jangle of keys, and finally the rattle of tumblers inside the lock on the front door.

"Tom? Tom?" Consuelo's whisper echoed down the hallway.

"Down here!" he replied as quietly as he could. "Don't light that lantern. Bring me the soldier's gun. Hurry!"

He could hear her sandals scraping across the dirt floor. It was too dark to see her face when she arrived at the door to his cell. She fumbled with the ring of keys, trying one, then another, until the lock turned.

He hurried out the door, bumping into Consuelo in the dark. She threw her arms around him. "Oh Tom!" she cried softly, burying her face against his chest.

"The gun!" he said sharply, pulling her arms away. "I've got to get my hands on that gun!"

He seized her by the hand and pulled her to the front door, where he paused briefly to peer around the door frame. By starlight, he could see Corporal Ramirez slumped against the adobe wall. Several hundred yards away, the lights of Guerrero shone brightly. He swung around the opening and knelt beside the soldier to pull his sidearm from its holster. Tom's hand closed around the butt of an ancient cap and ball revolver . . . he muttered a curse and stood up. The corporal's gun wouldn't be accurate beyond a few hundred feet, also requiring precious time to reload.

Consuelo rushed to his side. "The burro," she whispered, pointing to a dark arroyo west of town. "Follow me!"

"We need horses," Tom argued, glancing to the cantinas at the center of the business district. "Wait here. I'll fetch a couple of horses. If that soldier starts to wake up, bust his skull with a rock. Don't let him make any noise."

He took off toward town in a lumbering run, his legs weakened by bad food and his wound's slow recovery, gripping the old pistol in a sweat-dampened hand. Two people riding a burro across miles of rough desert stood no chance at all of making the border ahead of pursuit. It was a gamble Tom wasn't willing to take . . . not if he could get his hands on a couple of horses without being discovered.

He stumbled closer to the lights from a cantina, slowing to a walk when he reached the first of the abode huts at the edge of town. He could see the outlines of saddled horses standing at the hitchrail in front of the cantina. A few steps closer and he froze in his tracks when he glimpsed shadowy figures on the cantina porch, men wearing big sombreros idling away the cool night hours in front of the building.

Panting from his run, he clutched the corporal's pistol, weighing his chances. Trying to slip a pair of saddled horses away from one of the cantinas was too risky while men were watching the street. Left without a better selection, he turned away. He remembered the spot behind one cantina where Valdez kept the white stud. Trudging off in a different direction, he forced his leaden legs to carry him between the huts, hoping he wouldn't encounter any sleeping dogs that would sound an alarm. Once, he looked over his shoulder at the jail. No shadows moved near the adobe walls. For now, his escape went undetected.

He arrived at the rear of the cantina to find more disappointment. The white stallion wasn't there, nor were there any other horses. He stopped and caught his breath as a wave of dizziness weakened his knees. Too many days without sufficient food had robbed him of his strength. He was faced with just one chance to escape. The jackass Consuelo had hidden in the arroyo was his only hope.

Wheeling away from the back of the cantina, he forced his weary body into another effort to walk, though it felt as if his boots were mired in mud. His legs were trembling by the time he cleared the last of the small houses. Setting his sights on the jail, he stumbled onward, summoning all his endurance.

When he reached the corner of the jail, he collapsed on his rump beside the wall to catch his breath, groaning when he landed. Consuelo rushed to him from the doorway and knelt beside him.

"What is wrong, Tom?" she whispered, placing a hand on his chest.

"I'm too weak," he sighed. "Can hardly walk. We've got to drag that soldier inside and lock him in one of the cells. Tie him up and gag him so he can't yell for help when he wakes up. Help me get back on my feet. We're runnin' out of time."

She put his right arm around her neck and assisted him until he stood with his back against the wall. "Where will we find a rope?" she asked, glancing over to the slumbering corporal.

Tom's thoughts were too jumbled to answer her. He stuck the gun in the waistband of his denims and took uncertain steps toward the soldier. Bending down, he seized Ramirez's collar and started to drag him to the door. Consuelo took the corporal's arm and pulled with all her might. A few feet at a time, they pulled Ramirez into the dank darkness of the jail, then to the closest cell.

"Get the keys," Tom gasped, resting against the bars. "Tear some strips of cloth off your skirt so we can tie him. Then you'll have to go fetch that donkey. Don't think I can walk another step."

Consuelo brought the keys from the door to Tom's cell. She needed several seconds to find the key they required. When the cell door creaked open, she and Tom dragged the corporal inside. Moments later, he heard ripping cloth.

As weak as he was, it took valuable time to fasten the soldier's arms behind his back and stuff a gag into his mouth. When the chore was finished, Tom pulled himself up by the bars and staggered outside while Consuelo locked the cell, then the front door. Some of his strength had returned now.

"Let's head for that arroyo," he said hoarsely. "I'll walk as fast as I can."

Consuelo took his arm, steadying him as they started away from the building. His legs had turned to mush and it required every ounce of energy he had left to place one foot in front of the other. Now and then, he looked over his shoulder at Guerrero. Lights beamed from some of the windows in the business district, but the town was quiet.

In the pale starlight, he noticed the shredded remnants of Consuelo's skirt. Her heavy brown legs took long, purposeful strides beside him, assisting him across the uneven ground with some of his weight resting on her shoulder. If he could have found the strength to thank her, he would have spoken to her just then. For now, it was all he could manage to stumble forward.

It seemed an eternity before they started down a gentle slope into the arroyo. At the bottom of the dry wash, he saw the white muzzle and flip-flopping ears of the donkey, tethered to the trunk of a twisted mesquite bush. The animal raised its head to bray at them, when suddenly Consuelo rushed over to it, clamping her hand over the donkey's nostrils.

Tom staggered the last few steps to the burro's back, where he rested on his elbows, panting. "You'll have to help me up," he said between gasps for air.

Consuelo quickly untied the rope halter, then she hurried to Tom's side. She grasped his belt loops and gave a mighty heave. Her strength surprised him, for with almost no effort on his part he was aboard the donkey's back.

"Climb up behind me," he told her.

She shook her head, gathering the lead rope in her hands. "I will lead the burro," she whispered. "It will travel faster with a lighter load."

Consuelo led the burro off, angling northwest along the brushy bottom of the draw. Tom clung to the animal's scant mane with both hands, swaying back and forth with the donkey's gait, clamping its sides with his knees.

"Watch out for snakes," he said. "They'll be feeding at night, hot as it is."

She didn't answer him, leaning into a pull with the halter rope to hurry the donkey's footsteps as much as she could. At best, they would only move at a snail's pace, Tom knew. Nothing on earth would put haste into the steps of a jackass. They traveled at their own speed, no matter how much urging humans gave them.

The arroyo ended and they climbed to the desert floor. In the dark, cholla and yucca spines brustled like a thousand black daggers across the landscape. Ocotillo stalks pointed bony black fingers at the night sky as far as the eye could see in any direction. They would have to cross miles of this wasteland to reach the river.

For reassurance, he touched the handgrips of the old pistol. It wasn't much of a weapon against guns firing brass-jacketed shells. But if his adversaries got close enough, they would find themselves dodging low velocity balls of molten lead that would sever an arm or a leg rather than passing through cleanly. What mattered most was the fact that he was armed, regardless of the fashion. Even the bravest of men would think twice before closing in for a kill.

On level ground, Consuelo finally persuaded the donkey to break into a shuffling trot, requiring that she also trot among the thorny plants to keep pressure on the animal's rope. Tom drummed his heels against the donkey's sides. For a time, the little brown burro held the faster pace. Ultimately, the burro's disposition prevailed and it slowed to a walk, flipping its long ears back and forth in time with its strides. It was pointless to try to hurry the animal again.

Now and then, Tom glanced over his shoulder. There was no sign of pursuit. Traveling so slowly, he found it impossible to judge the distance they had covered. No matter how carefully he scanned the brushland before him, he saw no taller trees, the cottonwoods marking the winding course of the Rio Grande.

Later, he heard Consuelo gasping for breath. If he possessed the strength, he would have gladly walked while she rested on the burro's back. But when he tested his legs by clamping them around the donkey, he felt the weakness in them. Five days of dysentery had rendered him almost helpless.

"Hold up for a minute," he said, when Consuelo's breathing became more labored. "Take a rest. Nobody's behind us."

Consuelo shook her head. "I can rest when we cross the river," she replied. As though she found a new burst of energy, she leaned into a harder pull on the lead rope to hasten the donkey.

After another check of their backtrail, he thought about the dangers Consuelo had faced alone to come to his rescue. He would never have guessed that she felt so strongly about him. The cutting remarks she'd made about his age at the cantina didn't seem to fit the woman who was risking her life for him now, further convincing him that he would never understand women.

"Thanks for coming," he said weakly, knowing there were better words to express the way he felt, but without the ability to choose them. "The way it turns out, looks like you're about the best friend I've got. Makes me wish I hadn't said some of the things I did. I just want you to know . . .''

She stopped pulling on the rope and turned around to face him. The burro quickly came to a halt beside her. ''Jessie told me what you said,'' she began, puffing for wind between words. Beads of sweat clung to her face and arms. ''He told me that you wanted me to have your house, and half of the money under your mattress, if anything happened to you. Those words you said to Jessie filled my heart with happiness, Tom. Not for the house, or the money. I was happy because you care for me. Tears came to my eyes . . . tears of joy.''

He was deeply embarrassed, wishing Jessie had kept his mouth shut about Tom's private feelings. ''Jess shouldn't have told you that. Appears he's gettin' damn near as gossipy as Delia Cummings.''

Something made Consuelo glance over her shoulder. ''Jessie is waiting for us on the other side of the river with your horse. He told me about the *soldado* he shot. The *Federales* will hang him if he comes back to Mexico. He wanted to come. I made him promise to wait on the other side. We must hurry.''

She tugged the burro back to an ambling walk, aided by the drum of Tom's heels. Tom examined the horizon to the north, hoping for the sight of just one treetop that would announce their arrival at the Rio Grande.

Chapter Eighteen

The rumble of distant hoofbeats alerted him to the danger just as the burro entered the shallows on the Mexican side of the crossing. He whirled around and drew the cap and ball revolver from his waist. Gray dawn had just begun as a streak across the eastern sky. "Here they come," Tom growled. "Let go of that rope an' start swimmin'. Get out of the line of fire!"

"I will not leave you!" Consuelo shouted, throwing all her weight against the donkey's lead rope.

Tom's head snapped back to Consuelo. "Don't argue with me, you hardheaded bitch!" he cried, banging his bootheels into the burro's sides as hard as he could. "Get the hell outa the way! Lead's gonna be flyin' all over the place any minute now!"

He could see the hurt in her eyes, but there was no time to plead with her.

"I said get moving!" he barked angrily, pointing to the opposite bank.

When the water reached Consuelo's waist, she let go of the rope and started to swim. Her strokes were awkward, churning white foam across the surface. Splashing sounds followed the echo of Tom's harsh commands, drowning out the thunder of fast-moving horses coming from the south.

Tom turned back to the sloping riverbank where his pursuers would come into view. He raised the revolver to shoulder-height and thumbed back the hammer with a silent prayer that the caps would fire, and that his aim would be true. He hadn't fired a cap and ball since shortly after the war. The pistols were notoriously inaccurate. Confederate soldiers joked that the balls tumbled out of the muzzle, after powder rations were cut toward the close of the conflict.

Pounding the burro's ribs with his heels, he sighted along the riverbank. Dawn grayed the brush, playing tricks on his eyes. Water poured into his boots as the donkey neared the middle of the river. Now his legs were imprisoned by the water and he gave up the relentless kicking.

A horseman charged into plain sight on the low bluff above the river. Three more galloped closely behind.

"Allá! Allá!" a deep voice cried, as the first rider pointed down at Tom.

A gun crackled in the hand of one rider. A bullet hissed into the water on Tom's left, plowing a tiny furrow across the surface that gurgled and sputtered before it vanished. The sound made the burro lurch forward, almost spilling Tom from its back.

Another gun roared, accompanied by a stab of yellow flame that flickered and died. A slug whined above Tom's head. His targets were still out of range for the cap and ball, thus he had no choice but to wait, urging the donkey onward by clamping his legs against its sides. The four horseman raced down the gradual slope to the river. Among them, riding at the front on a lathered sorrel, was the *Federale* colonel, Comandante Ortega, waving a pistol above his head.

"Andale! Andale!" Tom was sure the command came from Ortega. He swung his gun sights to the colonel's chest and waited, lifting the muzzle slightly to allow for the drop of the ball when he fired.

The *comandante*'s sorrel charged down to the water's edge and sent up a shower of silver spray when its hooves struck the surface. The three men behind him reached the river at the same breakneck speed with guns held high, galloping their horses through the churning foam in the colonel's wake. Tom steadied his hand. A gunshot blasted from the gun of a rider on Ortega's flank. Tom tightened his finger around the trigger as a bullet sizzled overhead, harmlessly high. The burro gave another lunge and Tom was forced to wait, stiffening his arm until once again, Ortega filled his sights. He nudged the trigger, preparing himself for the brief delay after the hammer fell on the cap before the powder charge jolted his palm.

The hammer fell with a dull click. A cap had misfired. "Damn," he snarled, clenching his teeth as he drew the hammer back again. It required several seconds to steady his aim a second time. When he pulled the trigger, he felt a satisfying kick as the Colt bucked in his fist amid an earsplitting roar. Gunsmoke rolled away from the barrel, then he heard a cry. A rider behind Comandante Ortega was torn from the back of his horse, screaming in agony as he tumbled into the river. It was a lucky shot, aiming for Ortega like Tom was when he squeezed the trigger. He watched the riderless horse swerve.

A pistol spat flame, cracking like dry timber, while Tom was thumbing back the hammer for another shot. Angry shouts kept him from hearing the whine of the slug when one of Ortega's men spurred his horse to the front of the charge. Water crept over Tom's knees, for now the donkey struggled through the river's deepest mud. Sighting in on the closest horseman, he feathered the trigger gently, almost a caress. Exploding gunpowder drove the gun butt into his hand. A horse nickered in pain, then it stumbled, tossing the rider from its back. The ball had dropped just a fraction too much, striking the horse's neck. Silently, Tom cursed his aim.

From the Texas side of the river, a gun suddenly thundered to life, firing three shots in rapid succession. Tom whirled around to see who was doing the shooting, then he remembered that Jessie was waiting for them on the opposite bank with Tom's gelding.

A dark chestnut horse raced down to the crossing, its ears flattened on its neck, mane and tail flying. Jessie was bent low over the horse's withers, firing again and again as his chestnut bounded into the river. Tom's discovery was accompanied by relief and dread, for by Jessie's own admission, his aim was poor. A fourth shot banged from Jessie's gun. From the corner of his eye, Tom saw Consuelo floundering to shallower water, then he swung back to the south and drew a bead on the chest of a rider.

His gun roared and kicked. Comandante Ortega twisted sideways and grabbed his shoulder, dropping his pistol into the churning foam below his horse. Jessie's gun thundered again and the last of the four Mexicans jerked his mount to a halt. Ortega slumped over the pommel of his saddle, clutching his wound, when his horse suddenly shied. The *comandante* toppled sideways into the river, making a huge splash when he landed on the flat of his back. Behind Tom, Jessie fired once more and slowed his horse to a trot, then a walk through deeper water.

There was a moment of uneasy silence. The last Mexican remaining in the saddle reined his horse away. Ortega sputtered to the surface, coughing, swaying to find solid footing in water almost reaching his waist. He looked over his shoulder at Tom, taking his hand from his wound to shake an angry fist in the air. Between fits of coughing, he shouted something Tom couldn't quite hear.

Jessie's gelding reached the burro. The old cowboy was grinning when Tom turned around.

"I count three empty saddles!" he shouted, baring his gums when he said it, holding his pistol aloft. "No tellin' how many of 'em I shot! Things was happenin' too fast to count!"

Tom let his shoulders sag, flooded with relief now that the shooting had stopped. No purpose would be served by telling Jessie that every shot he fired was a miss. It was his bravery that counted most. "Figures you got most of 'em, Jess," he said. He showed Jessie the corporal's pistol. "This old cap an' ball can't hit the side of a barn. You saved my skin with some damn fancy shootin', pardner."

Jessie beamed, then his face turned serious. "I wanted to go back to Guerrero with Consuelo, but she argued that her plan was a hell of a lot better. I reckon she told you . . . I blowed a hole plumb through one of them *Federales* that night. He come 'round a corner of the cantina with his gun drawed. It was him or me, Tom. I shot him. An' when I run around to the front, I saw they had you out cold on the floor. Wasn't nothin' I could do against a room full of gun-totin' Mexicans. I ran for the horses. Been downright ashamed of myself ever since."

Tom urged the burro forward again, feeling tired enough to fall off the animal's back. "You showed good sense," he told Jessie, when the chestnut fell in beside the donkey. "No reason to feel ashamed of backing away from a fight you couldn't win."

Shafts of golden light spread across the eastern horizon as they rode slowly toward the riverbank. Tom saw Consuelo standing in ankle-deep water at the river's edge. When he looked closely, her wet blouse was clinging to her pendulous breasts, revealing every detail. Her skirt hung in shreds, plastered to her damp legs. He'd have seen little more of her if she were naked. He couldn't help but grin when he saw her in such disarray, her raven curls dangling limply to her shoulders. "Yonder's one hell of a brave woman," he said, turning to Jessie. "She may be a whore, but she's got more guts than most men I've known."

The burro and the horse sloshed through knee-deep current and the sounds muted Jessie's reply. "Whorin' ain't much different from most other professions," he said, turning a thoughtful glance to the sky. "Sellin' whiskey is sinful, accordin' to what Preacher Cummings preached, but there's a whole tubful of folks who run saloons, on account of there's so many folks with a thirst for it. A whore couldn't stay in the business for long without men willin' to pay for a poke. A man who'll bed down with a whore can't lay claim to bein' all that lily white. 'Bout the same as drinkin' Arturo's whiskey."

Jessie's logic made some sense, Tom supposed. Neither one of them could be called an expert on virtue. He guided the donkey over to Consuelo and slid off its back, casting a look over his shoulder. The mounted Mexican had jumped down to assist the *comandante* to dry land. One more of Oretega's men staggered drunkenly toward the bank with his hands pressed over his stomach. A pair of loose horses stood in the shallows with their heads lowered, gasping for wind.

When he looked down at Consuelo, he almost laughed, then caught himself. There was something in her eyes that made him forget her soaked appearance. She was staring at him, and he noticed that her bottom lip was trembling. He reached for her and took her in his arms. "We made it," he whispered, bending down to kiss her forehead. "This makes twice you saved my life. Don't hardly know the proper thing to say, except that I'm grateful. I won't forget what you've done for me."

She started to cry, with her face pressed against his chest. For a moment, her shoulders shook with silent sobs. She wound her arms around his waist and held him gently, careful not to put pressure near his wound. "I love you, Tom," she said quietly. "I have loved you for such a long time."

Tom looked over at Jessie, knowing he would never reveal his feelings while Jessie was around.

"I'll go fetch your horse," Jessie said, heeling his gelding to a walk. "It's tied over yonder in the brush." He swung the chestnut up the riverbank and rode over the crest of the rise.

Tom turned his attention back to Consuelo, wondering how to put his feelings into words. "I don't know a damn thing about love," he began, speaking softly. "Never was in love that I remember. Looks like I'd have known it, if I ever was. I reckon you could say I get attached to things I care about . . . that damned ol' spotted dog, my bay horse, good friends like Jessie. And you. Can't say that I'd call it love, really. I said some hard things to you a while back. Some of it mighty recent, I suppose. I cuss that dog damn near every day, but I don't mean a word of it. The dog knows it's just my way, to carry on like I was fixin' to bust a gut over somethin'. Sometimes a dog's got more sense than a human. Every time I cuss that dog, it wags its tail. Maybe it ain't payin' attention to the words, but it knows I got special feelings for it. Maybe that's what I'm tryin' to say to you. Don't pay a hell of a lot of attention to what comes out of my mouth . . ."

Consuelo drew her arms from his waist. Tears glistened in the corners of her eyes. She placed both palms against his cheeks, then stood on her tiptoes to kiss him.

He returned the kiss, until he heard Jessie coming back to the river with the horses. His hands dropped to his sides. "No sense actin' like a fool in front of Jess," he said quietly. He started up the bank with his boots sloshing full of river water.

When Consuelo was mounted on the donkey and Tom was seated in the borrowed saddle atop his bay, they started north. Across the Rio Grande, Ortega was being helped aboard his horse. Tom knew the affair was far from being over. The *comandante* would file a formal request to have Tom returned to Mexico, listing the same trumped-up charges as before, adding an escape from the Guerrero jail to his crimes. It would fall to the Texas

Rangers to handle the matter. He wondered what Captain Hardin would do about the incident.

When the river was out of sight behind them, Tom took stock of his condition. He was a free man, alive, suffering from a bad case of dysentery but still in one piece. His pride had suffered greatly at the hands of Luis Valdez and Colonel Ortega. He'd been humiliated a second time by Valdez, and his cattle were still in Mexico. It wasn't the sort of thing Tom could ignore. Making matters worse, he had lost his gun and holster to Ortega. Without his trusted single-action Colt .44 and the notched holster he was accustomed to, his draw would be slower.

"I've got to get my gun back, Jess," he said, thinking out loud as they crossed brushy flats away from the river.

Consuelo overheard the remark and spoke before Jessie had time to answer. "Why? You are safe now."

Tom set his chin, staring at the horizon. "Because the business between me an' Valdez ain't finished," he said quickly. "He's got my cows!"

"No, Tom!" she cried. "If you go back, they will kill you . . ."

He let a moment pass before he said any more. "There's some things a man just can't tolerate. One of 'em is bein' made to look like a damn fool. I'll pick the time and the place, but me an' Luis Valdez are gonna have a showdown, soon as I can figure a way to get my gun."

Jessie scratched his neck thoughtfully. "Don't see no way, Tom. Those *Federales* have got it. Besides, like Consuelo says, they'll kill you if you go back across that river."

Tom did not answer. A plan had begun to take shape in his mind. There was still the problem of the gun to be dealt with, but he was sure he knew a way to square things with Valdez where neither man had an advantage.

Chapter Nineteen

His strength had returned slowly, until he could walk about town without pausing for frequent rests. By the time the week was out, almost everyone around Rio Blanco had stopped by to see him and inquire about his health. Consuelo came to the house twice a day to prepare his meals and apply the salve to his wound. Jessie came late in the evenings to advise him about the condition of his cattle, which had only grown worse. Ranchers were starting to report dead cows near the shrinking waterhole in growing number. A roan cow of Tom's got bogged down in the mud, where she died before Jessie made his rounds. Talk down at the cantina centered around the grim prospects facing everyone who owned livestock. More wells in town had gone dry, like Tom's, including Benito's next door, forcing Tom to borrow water from Delia Cummings for himself and his horse. Tom tried to put the drought out of his mind, meeting with little success. The dry spell was on the tip of everyone's tongue. Chance Higgins announced that he was selling out. His cattle were starved down to walking skeletons and there was no relief in sight.

Tom kept himself occupied with his plan for revenge against Luis Valdez. In the privacy of his front room, he practiced his fast draw with Jessie's gun and holster. Jessie's Colt was an older single-action like Tom's, the type of gun Tom trusted. He'd offered Jessie fifty dollars for the pistol and belt, more than a fair price for an outdated weapon, in part to serve as a grubstake for the time when Jessie took off on his own to look for work. The holster required modifications, a latigo thong to tie it down to Tom's leg, and a deep notch cut out of the front so the gun barrel could begin its arc toward a target quickly. For days, Tom practiced inside the house without firing a single shot. Only when he was satisfied with the speed of his draw would it be necessary to fire at bottles on the stump. Hour after hour, he went into his crouch and drew the weapon, until the day came when he felt he was ready.

"Mornin', Miz Cummings," he said, tipping his hat politely as he walked toward the mesquite stump with an empty bottle. He was wearing his best Sunday hat now, for like his gun, he'd lost his everyday work hat the night his skull took the blow in Guerrero.

"You're not going to start that again, are you, Tom?" Delia asked, scowling at his gun.

"Yes ma'am, I surely am," he replied, continuing his march toward the stump. "Sorry to disturb your morning naptime. I'll only need a few minutes to get this gun sighted-in."

"A sensible person would have learned a lesson from your experience down in Mexico," she said sternly. "You're living in the past, Tom."

Without slowing his purposeful strides, he said, "I've never been accused of bein' sensible, Miz Cummings. I may be living in the past, like you claim I am, but it's just my nature not to abide a thief who steals my property. It may be old-fashioned to kill a man who steals, but that's what I aim to do." He arrived at the stump and put the bottle down, then he turned on his heel and began counting paces.

"You failed the last time," Delia remarked. "If that harlot hadn't come to your rescue, you'd still be in jail. I couldn't help but notice that you've taken to consorting with her again . . ."

Tom froze before he took the twelfth footstep, wheeling around to glare at Delia. "I reckon a harlot's the same thing as a whore," he snapped, losing the battle to control his temper. "There's no denyin' that whorin' is the way Consuelo makes her money. But she's one hell of a fine woman, braver'n most men in this town, and she don't stick her goddamn nose into everybody's business. It's my affair who I consort with. I'd be obliged if you stuck your snoot into somebody else's business besides mine. When I want your opinion, I'll ask for it. Now, go back inside, Miz Cummings. I'd hate for a stray bullet to wander through your bloomers by accident while I'm tryin' to get some practice."

Delia turned on her heel with a huff, then she paraded across her back porch and slammed the door behind her. Tom figured he had borrowed his last bucket of water from Delia's well after the things he said, but he consoled himself with the thought that the price had been too high anyway, enduring the lash of her tongue.

He resumed the measured paces until he reached thirty, allowing his anger to cool. When he turned around and sighted toward the stump he pushed everything else from his mind. With his hand poised above

213

the gun, he spread his feet apart and hunkered down. For a time he stood rock-still, tensing the muscles in his right arm.

"Now," he whispered, then he sent his hand downward, fingers acting reflexively, curling, closing around the grips. The barrel came up in its deadly arc, followed by an explosion.

He saw the tiny puff of dust beyond the stump and ground his teeth together. He'd missed badly. "Too damn high," he muttered, stabbing the Colt back in its holster. Jessie's pistol was lighter, a common fault he found with a Mason conversion. He hadn't compensated for the differences in weight. Tensing his arm again, he dipped his hand and pulled. The shot was high a second time, even higher than before.

Now he jammed the pistol into its leather berth and fixed the stump with an angry glare. He drew a third time, vowing to allow for the change in heft. The gun roared. He missed again, by a wider margin.

His fourth attempt also failed. As did the fifth, when his bullet struck the base of the stump with a resounding crack. He shook his head in disbelief, opening the loading gate to rod out the empty shells.

He was boiling mad at himself by the time the reloading was accomplished. Staring down at the gun, he said, "This damn thing'll get me killed."

Five more times, he reached for the Colt and drew as quickly as he could, until his ears were ringing from the noise. All five shots were wide of the target, some high, others low. When he holstered the gun for the last time, he let out a ragged sigh. "I've got to get my old gun back," he said softly. "Otherwise, I'm as good as dead."

He left the untouched bottle atop the stump and marched toward his house in a black mood, ignoring the people who had come outside to watch him shoot. He climbed the porch steps and went through the door, banging it shut behind him. Crossing to the bedroom, he went to a corner of his mattress and lifted it to pick up a yellowed envelope.

At the kitchen table, he poured himself a drink and sat down to spread the contents of the envelope before him. He emptied his glass and started to count the stack of dog-eared currency, knowing that when he came to the end of the tally, it would represent the sum of his life's work.

"Eleven hundred and forty-six dollars," he said softly, when the counting was done. The pile had shrunk considerably since the second year of the drought. The calves he sold lately were barely enough to cover his expenses. The last time he tallied the envelope, it held more than fifteen hundred hard-earned dollars.

He poured and drank again, after placing fifty dollars in a different stack. "That oughta do it," he told himself. He put the rest of the money back and carried it to the bedroom. With the fifty dollars in his pants pocket, he left the house to find Jesus Soto.

"Here's the message I want delivered," he said, holding the boy's attention with a raised finger. "You carry this money down to Guerrero and find Luis Valdez. Tell him that T.C. Culpepper has a proposition for him, a proposition that can make him a rich man. That'll get his interest. Tell him I'll wager a thousand dollars that I can beat him to the draw in a fair fight. I'll put the

215

money up with Colonel Ortega, so he'll know he can't be cheated. We'll stage the contest on the Mexican side of the crossing, on that flat bluff above the river. I want the *comandante*'s word that I won't be arrested. It'll just be me an' Valdez, to decide who's the better man with a gun.''

Jesus nodded, swallowing, his dark eyes rounding when he understood the nature of the message he would carry. *Sí,* Señor Tom,'' he replied in a strained voice.

''There's more,'' Tom continued. ''Valdez has to put up those stolen cows, and the big white stud. If I kill him, the cattle and the horse are mine. I want Ortega's promise that I can drive my livestock back across if I outgun Valdez. Make damn sure he understands that. I want his word that nobody'll bother me if I'm the winner. If Valdez is faster, he'll be richer by a thousand dollars. That's a hell of a lot of money.''

Jesus nodded again. ''I will remember everything,'' he said. ''I will explain it very carefully. If Señor Valdez agrees, I will ask him to write down his promise, so you will know he understands.''

''That's a good idea, Jesus,'' Tom agreed. ''Have the comandante sign it, too. Tell them the date is set for next Sunday . . . that's the first Sunday in September, in the afternoon. Three o'clock sounds good to me. I'll send the money across just as soon as Valdez shows up with those cows and the horse. Ortega can give me a signal when he's satisfied.''

Jesus looked down at his boots. Tom knew the boy had something on his mind.

''Why are you doing this, Señor Tom?'' he asked.

''It's a matter of honor,'' he answered. ''Valdez is a prideful man. He'll understand. He made me look like a damn fool in front of my friends. I want the chance to get even.''

Jesus turned for his pony and stuck a foot in the stirrup.

"Just one more thing," Tom remarked, as he took the fifty dollars from his pocket. "The deal's off unless I can buy back my gun and holster. You tell them that, too. Offer Ortega fifty dollars for my Colt and the belt. That's twice what it's worth to anybody else.''

Jesus took the money.

"There's an extra five dollars there for you," Tom added. "Now get goin', and don't forget anything I said. Stop by the house as soon as you get back, so I'll know what Valdez had to say.''

The boy mounted and gathered his reins. "I will remember," he replied. He swung his pony away from Tom's porch and heeled it to a trot.

Tom watched Jesus until he disappeared into the brush below Rio Blanco. "Valdez will take my proposition," he said quietly, an eye on the dust cloud moving toward the southern horizon. "He'll do it for the money. There ain't a gunslinger livin' who don't have his price . . .''

He turned back to the house when the dust was gone, to open a fresh bottle of whiskey and wait for Jesus to return. Tom was staking everything he owned on the outcome of a gun battle, a foolish notion until you considered something called pride. On the ride back to Rio Blanco after the jail break, he'd made up his mind. In his heart, he knew he would rather be dead than disgraced for the balance of his lifetime. Under the best of circumstances, he didn't have that many years left to him. The long dry spell had ruined his chances to live comfortably to old age, and if couldn't have his dignity, he'd be nothing but a shell of a man until he went to his grave. It was better to die with a fistful of blazing iron, for the chance to preserve his honor.

He uncorked a bottle and drank deeply. The house was hot on this windless afternoon, thus he carried the whiskey out on the porch and settled into his chair. The dog left its shady spot and came over to him, wagging his tail, placing its chin on Tom's leg to be petted.

"Worthless hound," he muttered, rubbing the dog's neck, his mind elsewhere. He tried to visualize the showdown beside the river. In his daydream, people had come from miles around to witness the duel. Surrounded by crowds of bystanders, he saw himself glowering at Valdez, hand poised above his gun. In his mind's eye, he saw the draw he would make, a sure-handed move toward the Colt, the pull, then the shot.

"I can beat him," he said to himself.

He drank again, savoring the sweet taste of good barley mash, when the vision evaporated. Until Sunday, he woudn't think abut anything else, not the drought, nor dying longhorns, or dry wells. He wouldn't allow Delia Cummings to get under his skin either. For the rest of the week, he would concentrate on the forthcoming gunfight and nothing else.

Later he dozed, resting his head against the wall. Just before he drifted off, he made up his mind to visit the cantina tonight, after it got cooler. Consuelo would like that. Everyone would know their feud was over.

The click of horseshoes startled him. When he opened his eyes, he saw Jessie coming toward the house at a trot. Fearing bad news, Tom took several swallows of whiskey, waiting for Jessie to arrive.

"Evenin', Tom," Jessie said, swinging down tiredly,

then knocking the dust from his clothing by fanning his hat. "Dry as popcorn in the south pastures."

Tom made a face. "Hardly expected to hear it had turned into a swamp, Jess. Tell me somethin' I didn't already know."

Jessie climbed the porch steps and took the bottle Tom offered. "I counted nine dead sheep today," he began, pausing long enough to fill his mouth with whiskey. He swallowed and drew in a quick breath when he felt the burn. "Two more dead cows . . . wasn't none of 'em yours, and nine sheep. The damn vultures are thick as flies on a pile of dog shit down yonder. Can't hardly see the sun no more. I reckon Pedro Flores will feel the pinch right soon. He ain't got all that many sheep to start with."

Tom wanted to talk about something else, almost anything else besides dead livestock. "I sent word down to Luis Valdez that I'd meet him face to face this comin' Sunday. Offered him a thousand dollars against my cows and the white stud, winner takes all."

Jessie frowned. "You right sure you want to go through with it?" he asked, knocking back another drink.

"Damn right I'm sure," he answered quickly, to dispel any doubt in Jessie's mind. "I can beat him. I just know I can."

Jessie handed back the bottle, shaking his head. "Sorta wish you wouldn't. Valdez might get lucky . . ."

Tom gazed across the sun-baked land, looking at nothing in particular. "My mind's made up," he said in a faraway voiced. "Come Sunday, I'll prove I'm not too old to handle a gun. I'm bettin' everything I have that I'm faster."

219

Jessie sighed. "Where'll you do it?" he asked.

"At the river crossing. On the Mexican side, where the Rangers can't interfere." He squinted at a dust devil, thinking about the duel. A gentle breeze swept across the porch, smelling of dust.

Chapter Twenty

Lantern globes cast flickering shadows across the floor of the cantina. Tom sat at his favorite corner table. A bowl of salted limes sat before him, next to a bottle of tequila with almost half its contents missing. The hour was late and most patrons had headed for home. Consuelo was washing glasses in the kitchen while Arturo applied raw candellia wax to the top of his wooden bar. The place had been unusually quiet tonight. Conversation centered around the dying animals and dry wells of Rio Blanco, grim topics no one really wanted to discuss. Tom had paid little attention to the talk, waiting to hear the message Jesus brought back from Guerrero. And the longer he waited, the more restless he became. Where the hell was Jesus?

Consuelo came from the back and started extinguishing the lanterns. She saw the question on Tom's face. "It is past midnight," she said softly.

He got up and placed coins on the table. Consuelo came over to meet him at the door before he walked out.

"Something is troubling you," she insisted, touching his sleeve gently.

He took a deep breath. "I sent Jesus down to Guerrero with a message for Valdez," he began. "I'm putting up damn near everything I've got to challenge him to a contest of the draw this comin' Sunday. No word yet from Jesus about my proposition. I hope the boy's all right . . ."

"No, Tom," she whispered, tugging his sleeve now. "Please don't do this. Please!"

"It's somethin' I've gotta do," he told her. "I've got to know who's faster . . . who's got the better aim. He made me the laughing stock of this town. I won't live the rest of my life lookin' like some damn fool. I'd just as soon be dead as laughed at. It may not make any sense to you, but it does to me."

She reached for his face and touched his cheek tenderly, her eyes suddenly brimming with tears. "I try to understand," she said. "I try . . ."

He bent down and kissed her lightly. "Don't worry. I can handle myself. Good night, Consuelo. I've got to wait up for Jesus."

He clumped off into the dark, looking south, toward the Mexican border. "Sure as hell hope nothing's happened to that boy," he whispered.

An hour later, as he sat on the porch sipping whiskey, he heard distant hoofbeats. The dog got up and whimpered, looking to the south.

"That'll be Jesus," he told himself, leaning forward in his chair. He listened to the drum of hooves. Some of the worry left him.

Jesus trotted his pony up to the house and swung down. He pulled off his straw sombrero and took a piece of paper from his shirt pocket. "Señor Valdez agrees to your conditions," he said, handing Tom the folded

222

foolscap. "He says he will meet you at the river on Sunday. The cows will be there. He will ride the *caballo blanco*. If you kill him, you have only to take the animals. He has placed his *firma* on the paper. Comandante Ortega did also, to say he agrees to your terms. You will not be arrested . . . he swore an oath to the Virgin Mary, señor. He also laughed," Jesus added quietly.

"What made him laugh?" Tom asked, opening the paper even though it was too dark to read.

Jesus cleared his throat. "He called you *viejo loco,* señor. He told everyone that you would . . . die."

"What about my gun?" Tom asked, looking past the boy to the saddle on the pony's back.

Jesus whirled around, mumbling an apology, "I forgot, Señor Tom," as he took the cartridge belt from his saddle horn. "The *comandante* also laughed when I made the offer of fifty dollars for your gun. Senor Valdez, he laughed, too, making everyone at the cantina laugh with them."

Tom stood up when he took the gun and holster, examining it briefly in the starlight. He closed his right hand around the butt of the Colt and pulled it from the holster. "Let 'em have their laugh," he said, as a slow smile crossed his face. "Let 'em laugh all the way to Sunday. The laughin' will stop around three o'clock Sunday afternoon . . ."

Jesus waited beside his pony, until Tom remembered he was standing there.

"You did a good job, Jesus," he remarked. "I'm obliged."

Jesus bowed politely and swung in the saddle. *"Buenas noches,"* he began. "I, too, am grateful, for the money you paid me. You are very generous, Señor

223

Tom." He wheeled the pony away and kicked it to a lope away from the house.

Tom turned for the door and went inside. He lit the lantern on the kitchen table and spread the piece of paper before him, adding his Colt .44 to the spot. Frowning, he read each word slowly to himself. The scrawl was fuzzy even at arm's length, thus he read carefully until he reached a pair of signatures at the bottom. Some of the words were written in Spanish, but the meaning was clear. Luis Valdez and Filemon Ortega agreed to his terms. Ortega would hold the money until the duel was decided. The winner received everything. Tom was satisfied.

He looked down at the gun. "Here's where you made your biggest mistake," he said softly, picking up the pistol, resting it in the palm of his hand. "For fifty dollars, you just sold yourself a trip to the undertaker's for Luis Valdez. Take a good look at the sunrise this Sunday mornin', Luis, 'cause it's the last one you'll ever see."

He took off the gunbelt he bought from Jessie and strapped on his own. Then he dropped the Colt into its holster and turned away from the table. He waited a few seconds, watching his shadow on the wall dance with false life provided by the flame. Ever so slowly, he crouched down and tensed his right arm.

A muffled gunshot brought Delia Cummings flying off her mattress, jolted wide awake from a sound sleep. She grasped one post of her four-poster bed to steady herself, cocking an ear toward the noise. "It's that Tom Culpepper again," she told herself in a shaky voice, trying to calm her nerves. "Now the old fool's taken to shooting practice in the dark. He has lost his mind completely. If I could sell this house I'd move to the middle of Hades itself to get away from him." She looked up at the ceiling. "Forgive me, Lord, for saying such a thing, but the man's gone stark raving mad. Half the time he forgets his pants when he walks outside. A time or two, I've seen him relieve himself off the back porch in broad daylight. He uses the worst profanity, even when he's only talking to that poor dog!"

She slumped to the edge of her bed to await the next volley of gunfire, knowing it would be impossible to sleep. "He can't see that bottle at all," she whispered later. "He'll be shooting all night, I suppose. There ought to be a law, that when a person loses his mind he can't own a gun . . ."

Dawn came clear and dry to Rio Blanco. Benito's rooster crowed a greeting to the rising sun just below Tom's bedroom window, which evoked a muffled curse when Tom heard it, lifting his head from his pillow sleepily to see if somehow the chicken had managed to get inside his house to deposit its droppings and squawk.

He sat up and rubbed sleep from his eyes, then he swung his bare legs off the bed. The rooster crowed again. "The son of a bitch," he muttered, scowling at the window, envisioning mountains of droppings below the windowsill. "If I had a dog that wasn't so goddamn lazy . . ."

He pushed himself up and padded slowly toward the kitchen to start a fire in the stove. Consuelo brought coffee beans the week before and if there was any water left in the bucketful he'd borrowed from Delia, he could boil coffee. At the drainboard, he inspected the bucket and grunted happily, despite a headache from last night's tequila and whiskey. Opening the cast-iron door to the firebox, he tossed in a few mesquite splits and struck a match, begging a flame to life by blowing on it gently. When the fire was underway, he took a few dippers of water and combined them with beans in the coffeepot. As he turned away from the stove, he saw a shaft of sunlight coming through a hole in the east wall of the house.

"Right through the heart," he remembered. He'd fired at his shadow last night, and his aim had been perfect.

The rooster cackled and he was sure the sound came from his front porch. He glanced to the gunbelt hanging from the back of a chair. "That does it, you feathered bastard," he growled, hurrying to the chair to draw the .44. "I won't tolerate chicken shit on my front porch," he added, making for the door clad only in his underwear.

When he walked outside, he spotted the rooster pecking the hardpan a few yards from the corner of his house. He considered the wisdom of killing the chicken then and there. Everyone on this side of town would run outside to see who was shooting, and then he'd have to explain away the death of Benito's rooster.

He glanced toward Benito's house, and saw Mrs. Sanchez hanging clothes on her clothesline. If he killed the rooster now, there was a witness. He relaxed his grip on the gun and glared at the sleeping dog near the edge of the porch. "You're worthless," he spat, shaking his head.

The sound of his voice awakened the dog. It raised its chin off its front paws and yawned, wagging its tail.

The indifferent yawn was more than Tom could stand. He wheeled around and stalked back inside, banging the door shut behind him. After holstering the gun, he went to the bedroom to dress, cheered a little by the aroma of coffee. When he was fully attired in denims, a bib shirt, and boots, he walked to the wardrobe and examined his black broadcloth suit for food stains and wrinkles. He meant to wear the suit on Sunday, along with a freshly boiled white shirt and the last of his paper collars. He hadn't needed his churchgoing attire since Reverend Cummings died. Not since the funeral. But this Sunday, he would be dressed in his best for the meeting with Valdez.

He returned to the kitchen table to await his morning coffee, but when he spied the half-finished bottle of whiskey, he sloshed some into his cup and took a tentative sip, then another. As soon as the warmth spread to his belly he abandoned the notion of having any of the coffee at all. He drained the cup and poured again before getting up to take the pot off the stove.

On his way to the front door with the cup of whiskey, he stopped to strap on his gunbelt. Hardly a day had passed in the last twenty-five years that he didn't wear it. It felt good to have it on again.

Out on the porch, he eased into his chair. The dog came over, yet he barely noticed. His eyes were fixed on the southern horizon, where five days hence, he would pit his skill as a gunslinger against one of northern Mexico's most feared *pistoleros*. Thinking this, he smiled.

Chap Grant and Hank Wardlaw rode dust-caked horses toward the house. Tom leaned forward in his chair, wondering if the pair meant to pay him a social call. The men halted their mounts in the yard and stepped down. Hank was looking straight at Tom when he tied off his reins, but Chap averted his eyes, making Tom suspect the reason for their visit.

"Afternoon, Tom," Hank said, climbing to the porch to shake hands. "You're lookin' better. Got some of your color back."

Tom merely grunted and took the handshake.

"Howdy, Tom," Chap intoned, wearing a half-hearted grin when they shook, then he looked down at his boots.

Hank hooked his thumbs in his front pockets. "We rode over to try an' talk some sense into you," Hank began, evidently appointed as spokesman for the pair. "Jesus told Chap about that offer he took down to Guerrero. He made mention of that paper Valdez signed, and the thousand dollars you intend to put up as your part of the wager. It's a plumb stupid idea, Tom. Dumbest thing I've ever knowed you to do. We've been neighbors and friends for nigh onto twenty years now, and this is the craziest stunt you've ever pulled. Chap has knowed you most all his life, and you were a good friend to Chap's pa before he died. Me an' Chap decided we'd try to change your mind about it."

Tom shook his head. "You've wasted a ride to town, if that's why you came," he said evenly.

Chap made an effort to square his shoulders. "We're your friends, Tom. We hoped you'd listen to reason."

In reply, Tom shrugged. "Ain't neither one of you said nothin' reasonable yet. It's my money. Worked most of my life for it, so I can damn well do whatever I please with it."

"It's crazy," Hank protested, raising his voice. "Just what the hell do you figure you're gonna prove?"

At that, Tom got out of his chair, so he could look Hank and Chap in the eye. "I'll prove I ain't a damn coward," he answered flatly, turning to Chap. "It proves I've got the guts to go after what's mine."

Hank adopted a pleading tone. "Nobody's ever questioned your courage, Tom. There ain't hardly a soul in this county who wouldn't swear you're the toughest hombre in these parts. But what you're doin' now don't make any sense. Hell, the gunfightin' days are over. And those damn scrawny longhorns ain't worth a thousand dollars, maybe not even half that much. They sure as hell ain't worth a good man's life. Are you listenin' to me, Tom?"

"Heard every word you said plain as day," he replied. "There ain't a damn thing wrong with my ears."

Hank's expression turned blank. "Then how come you ain't agreein' with what I just said?" he asked.

Tom waited a moment to give his answer, measuring what he would say. Hank and Chap had come as friends. He meant to avoid hurting their feelings if he could, especially Hank's. "There's some folks around here who've forgotten some mighty important things about bein' a rancher in this part of Texas. Back when times were rough, we all stuck together. We never let anybody push us. We claimed this country and held onto it, with guns when we had to. Nobody ever crossed this range and took what was ours." Then he paused, moving his gaze to the horizon. "Everybody keeps sayin' how times have changed, and I reckon maybe they have. But there's one thing that don't ever change in my book . . . what a man does when it's time to stand up and be counted.

229

When a bunch of thievin' Mexicans steal cows from our herds, I say it's time to show 'em we ain't yellow. To hell with a law that says I can't cross that river to take back what they stole from me, and when those uppity sons of bitches came back to try it again, not a soul would back my play to try to stop 'em. So I've made up my mind to do it myself. I'm gonna kill Luis Valdez in a fair fight . . . give him the first pull, fight him on his own ground. When I'm done, I'll come back with our rustled livestock. Just as important, the next son of a bitch who thinks about tryin' it again will know he'll have to deal with me.''

Chap's face had turned red. ''You're talkin' about me, ain't you?'' he asked. ''You figure I shoulda gone down there with you the first time . . .''

He looked at Chap for a while, remembering Chap's father, thinking how much the boy favored him. ''I was disappointed when you didn't go,'' he said. ''Your pa would have been right there beside me. I understand you've got a family to raise, but so did your pa, back then, and he never once backed away from trouble. I'm not holdin' it against you, Chap. We're still friends.''

Now it was Hank's turn to look down at his boots. ''If it hadn't been for Consuelo, you'd still be down there in that jail. You bucked the odds when you an' Jessie rode to Guerrero. You're a lucky man to be free of those bars.''

Tom studied Hank's face. ''Sometimes, a feller has to count on a piece of luck. That, and a little bit of help from his friends now and then.''

Hank's shoulders sagged. ''You've made it real plain there's no talking you out of meetin' Valdez, so I reckon we'll go. I couldn't have looked myself in the mirror unless I tried to make you see things my way. Be seein' you, Tom. Time we headed back.''

Hank swung off the porch, but Chap hesitated, scuffing a boot toe absently. "Sorry I disappointed you," he said softly, without looking up. "I ain't the same as my pa. My family means more to me than my cows. Shucks, I figure this will be my last year in the cattle business anyway, if it don't rain.''

Tom clapped Chap on the shoulder. "No need to apologize," he said. "Come Sunday, I'll put a stop to the rustlin' around here when I put Valdez in his grave.'' He looked up at the sky. "It'll rain pretty soon. Your pa would have wanted you to stay on the ranch. Don't let a few dry years force you out. Things are gonna change, just you wait and see.''

Chap nodded and went down the steps with his hands shoved in his pockets. Tom watched them mount their horses. He waved when they reined back toward town. He hadn't wanted to say so in front of Hank, but he was disappointed with him, too. Before the drought broke his spirit, Hank had been as tough as boot leather. It was a damn shame how a dry spell changed him.

Chapter Twenty-One

He stood a good distance from the mirror to admire his reflection, beginning with his hat. He'd dusted it off before daylight, and applied boot black to his boots. Consuelo had come over after the cantina shut down, to trim his hair with her scissors. After the haircut, she had cried in his arms and begged him not to keep the appointment with Valdez today. Later, he'd surrendered to urges and taken her to his bed. It had seemed different this time, unlike the business proposition it had been before.

He examined the stiff paper shirt collar and his silk string tie, then the split-tail black coat. His pants were stuffed into the tops of his stovepipe boots. He decided he looked more like a gambler, or a preacher just now, unless you noticed the bulge of the gun underneath his coat. When he was satisfied with his appearance, he took off his hat to run a comb through his newly shorn locks. He added a dash of bay rum tonic to his hair, then he replaced the hat, pulling the brim low in front before he left the bedroom to sit on the porch.

Resting a half-empty whiskey bottle on his knee, he

touched the envelope in his coat pocket, leaning back in his chair with his gaze fixed on the southern horizon. His bay stood hipshot at one corner of the porch with Hank's saddle cinched to its back. Everything was ready. He patted the butt of his gun absently. Last night, he'd given it another good cleaning and a coat of oil.

"Today's the day," he said, to himself. The dog whimpered when it heard his voice, asking to be petted. Without looking down, he scratched the dog's ears and took a big swallow of whiskey.

A commotion in town drew his attention to Main Street. Chance Higgins drove his wagon past the *mercado*. His wife sat beside him on the wagon seat. Tom wondered why they had come to town on Sunday. Chance halted his team of razor-thin mules in front of the cantina. Dust settled around the wagon, then Chance jumped down to assist his wife to the ground.

The first gusty notes from Delia's pump organ ended the silence abruptly, a reminder that it was eleven o'clock on Sunday morning. Tom came to his feet slowly. It was time to head for the river. He glanced down at the dog. "If I don't make it back, you're on your own," he said. "I don't figure anybody else will feed you. I'd consider it a personal favor if you'd kill that damn red rooster. I'd be a hell of a lot happier restin' in my grave, knowin' that chicken took his last shit in my yard."

He drank again and went down the steps, corking the bottle before he put it in a saddlebag. The bay swished away a fly with its tail while he was mounting. When he swung away from the house, he saw Maria hurrying toward him from the middle of town. She was wearing her best dress, made from a bolt of bright blue cloth that had arrived in Rio Blanco the week before, along with the shipment of coffee. She saw Tom and waved, running harder. She was out of breath by the time she reached him. Tom noticed a strange look on her face, different from her usual warm smile.

"I came to wish you *buena suerte,* Señor Tom," she said. *"Vaya con Dios."* She reached out to touch a leg of his pants gently.

He smiled down at her. "I'll have good luck today," he reassured her. "I can feel it all the way to my toes."

"I'll be watching," she said timidly. "I will be praying for you. And so will Consuelo."

His smile became a frown. "You're not goin' down there . . . it ain't the sort of thing a woman oughta watch."

She curtsied, a curious thing to do right then. "We are all going in Señor Higgins's wagon. Thank you, for calling me a woman. Always before, you tell me I am only a little girl."

"You shouldn't go," he protested, glancing to the wagon, where several people were gathered . . . Pedro Flores and his wife, Benito Sanchez, his wife and children, Arturo Benevides holding the reins to a saddled burro, the Delgado family. And Consuelo, wearing her bright yellow skirt with a piece of yellow ribbon in her hair.

"Almost everyone is going," Maria said. "Only Señora Cummings refused the invitation to ride in the wagon."

"That don't surprise me," he replied, listening to the wheeze of Delia's organ as it pumped forth a hymn he didn't recognize. "I still say the women hadn't oughta see a killing," he added softly.

He touched the brim of his hat to Maria and heeled the bay to a trot. From the corner of his eye, he saw Consuelo wave to him. He waved back, then quickly turned his attention to the lay of the land in front of him, noting that there was no wind today. It was as if the Almighty were holding His breath on this particular Sunday.

A sizable group of horsemen were gathered on the Texas side of the crossing. Tom rode toward them, puzzled by their presence. He recognized Hank Wardlaw and his sons first, then Jessie Kootz. Chap Grant and Jesus Soto were there. Two strangers seemed to be the center of attention. But when Tom rode closer, he recognized the pair. Ranger Captain Bob Hardin and his deputy sat their horses near the crossing, watching Tom ride down to the river. Judging time by the angle of the sun, it was almost three o'clock. When Tom looked across the river, to the bluff on the Mexican side, he saw a sight that he had not expected. A crowd of at least a hundred people waited near the spot where Tom and Valdez would meet. Most of the men wore straw sombreros, while the women were dressed in bright colors, some shielding their faces from the sun with ornamented shawls. To the east, a herd of longhorns bawled for water as three *vaqueros* drove them closer to the river.

Tom slowed his bay to a walk, for at the edge of the crowd on the Mexican side, he saw Luis Valdez aboard the prancing white stud. Valdez wore a pale gray felt sombrero. Glittering silver conchos decorated the crown of his hat, sparkling in the afternoon sun.

"Looks like he wore his Sunday best," Tom muttered. He turned his gaze back to the two Rangers. Were they here to try to stop the duel? They had no legal authority in Mexico, so why were they here?

He rode up to the group waiting at the river, nodding politely to each of his friends. Then he looked at the Rangers, waiting for the captain to speak.

"Afternoon, T.C.," Hardin said. Dick Cole simply nodded once. "We got word there was fixin' to be a killin' here today."

Tom took his eyes off the Rangers to scan the opposite bank for a moment. "There is," he replied, dry-voiced, when his gaze came to rest on the figure atop the nervous white horse.

It seemed Hardin was waiting for Tom to explain. When Tom offered nothing more, the Ranger said, "It ain't gonna happen here."

Off to the north, Tom could hear the rattle of Chance's wagon. The mules had been driven hard to arrive so quickly. "I understand," he replied to the captain's warning. "It's set for the Mexican side. You got nothin' to worry about."

"We had to make sure," Hardin continued. "Comes with the badge."

Tom agreed silently, inclining his head.

Deputy Cole had a ball of tobacco in his mouth, making his cheek appear swollen. He spat on the ground below a stirrup and spoke to Tom, his words mushy. "Never met a feller in such a hurry to get himself killed, Culpepper. There's enough Meskins over yonder to start another revolution. If you get lucky enough to shoot the old bastard named Valdez, his friends will gun you down a'fore you can sneeze. Appears you need some lessons in 'rithmatic. There's fifty men on the other side of that river.''

Tom tried to hide his impatience with the deputy. ''There's a thing called honor. Valdez is a *pistolero*. This thing's just between him'n me.''

Cole wagged his head, like he didn't believe it. ''Them's old-fashioned ideas. His *amigos* will kill you, if you're fast enough to get off the first shot.''

''Maybe,'' Tom answered, tired of wasted words. He turned to Jesus and reached for the envelope in his coat pocket. ''Take this over to Colonel Ortega. Tell him to give me a signal after he's counted it.''

Jesus nudged his pony alongside Tom's bay. The boy's face was drained of color when he took the envelope. *''Sí*, Señor Tom.'' His hand was trembling when he stuck the money inside his shirt.

Tom watched Jesus ease his pony into the shallows, then he fixed a stare on the far side of the river where Valdez held the sidestepping stallion in check. Not far away, Colonel Ortega sat quietly on a big buckskin gelding with his arm in a white cloth sling.

''Don't go, Tom,'' Hank implored. ''There's still time to call the boy back with the money. There ain't a soul in Rio Blanco who'd think any less of you if you gave up on this crazy idea.''

The wagon bounced and creaked to a halt behind him before he gave Hank his reply. ''You know I can't do that, Hank,'' he said quietly.

Hank bowed his head and closed his eyes.''Damn, Tom. You've got too damn much pride for your own good.''

He heard the patter of sandals coming toward him from the rear. When he turned around, he saw Con-

suelo. Tears streamed down her face, making little damp circles on the front of her blouse that made it appear she'd been out in a rainstorm. She stopped when she reached his left stirrup and gazed up at him. Though she made no sound, her shoulders shook with silent sobs.

"Adiós," she whispered, placing a hand on his knee gently.

His throat was unaccountably tight and he didn't answer her. He shook his head and turned back to the river, just as Jesus trotted his water-soaked pony up the gentle slope to the bluff. He felt Consuelo take her hand away, but he wouldn't look at her.

Jesus rode past the clusters of bystanders until he arrived in front of Colonel Ortega. Tom saw him hand the *comandante* the envelope and then back his pony away.

Ton turned his attention to Valdez. The white stud had settled and now it stood quietly. Valdez's face was aimed in Tom's direction. "He's lookin' me over," Tom whispered to himself. "Wonderin' if he can take me . . ."

Slowly, as the men stared at each other, a curious calm spread through Tom. He likened the feeling to a big drink of whiskey.

Jessie reined his horse over, catching Tom's eye. "Soon as you kill him, me an' some of the boys will head over to circle them cows. Won't take us long to cross 'em. If I was you, I wouldn't stay over yonder 'til my beard started to grow."

Tom opened his mouth to object, when Colonel Ortega stood in his stirrups and waved a hand over his head. "There's the signal," Tom said. "You stay here, Jess. Ortega might still be on the prod over that Federale you shot. Send somebody else." He clamped his heels against the bay's ribs and rode down to the Rio Grande.

He reached the middle of the river before he noticed movement on the bluff. Colonel Ortega trotted his horse toward the crossing. Tom frowned. Even though the *comandante* was alone, he started to worry about a double cross. Jesus reined his pony into the shallows on the Mexican side. Tom waited until the boy came alongside his bay. Jesus spoke before Tom could frame a question.

"The *comandante* wishes to speak to you," he said, glancing over his shoulder.

"Hurry your pony across," he replied. Farther downstream, he could see the longhorns grouped on the riverbank.

Jesus lashed his pony's rump with his reins. The little sorrel lunged into deeper water. Tom swept his coat tail behind the butt of his Colt and urged the bay forward again.

Colonel Ortega arrived at the edge of the river and halted his horse, waiting for Tom to negotiate the shallows. As soon as Tom was within hearing distance, Ortega spoke.

"We meet again, Señor Culpepper," he said, cracking a mirthless grin.

Tom stopped the bay in front of the colonel's buckskin. "The boy said you wanted a word with me."

Ortega nodded, patting the front of his tunic. "The money is here," he said. "If you are faster than Luis, you can reclaim it." He ran a fingertip across his thin mustache. "The cattle as well, and the stallion." Now his expression changed, his black eyes alive with hatred. "I could have you shot, señor, for making the escape from my jail, and for the bullet you put in my arm." The false smile returned to his mouth. "However, I have given my word and signed my name to the paper. If you survive the pistol duel with Luis, you will be allowed to return to Texas. Of course, I do not truly believe you are faster than the great Luis Valdez. He will most certainly kill you. Of that, I am sure.''

Ortega swung his horse around and started back up the bank. Tom let the bay have its head and followed to the top of the bluff. When he reached level ground, he looked across the flat plain at Valdez. The gunman was watching him. A hush fell over the crowd. Women and children began to back away. The men behind Valdez moved off to be out of the line of fire. Three hundred yards separated them now, as they stared at each other. Tom halted his horse and swung his right boot over its rump to reach the ground.

He dropped one rein to ground hitch the gelding, then he started walking forward. Valdez saw Tom dismount and stepped down. A soldier in a blue tunic hurried over to take the stud's reins. As soon as the horse was led away, Valdez started toward Tom.

The silence on the bluff was absolute. Tom could hear the Mexican's silver spurs rattle as they came closer together. Sunlight caught on the row of silver conchos around Valdez's somberero, shimmering. He was dressed in leather leggings, a black vest, and a silky white shirt with billowy sleeves that fluttered as he walked. For the duel, he had discarded the cartridge belts across his chest. A single bullet would settle matters between them, making the bandoleers useless.

At a hundred yards, Tom slowed his footsteps. Valdez saw this and shortened his strides, inching his hands closer to the pair of pistols. Tom wondered which gun he favored, the left, or the right, when he made his move toward a weapon.

241

At fifty yards, Valdez halted. Tom could see the streaks of gray in his beard. He continued moving closer until he judged the distance to be right. Thirty paces from his adversary, Tom stopped and spread his feet apart, tensing his right arm.

A gust of unexpected wind swept the bluff, ruffling Valdez's sleeves. They stared at each other, neither man moving. Somewhere in the crowd, an infant started to cry until it was silenced by its mother.

"Make your move, Valdez," Tom said. "Like I told you before, the first pull is yours."

At that, Valdez smiled. "You are, indeed, *un pendejo,* to give me the advantage."

"Maybe," he replied. "It's the way I conduct my business."

The gunman's smile faded, becoming a snarl. His shoulders bunched imperceptibly, merely a tiny ripple inside his shirt.

He's ready now, Tom thought. I've got to keep my eyes on both hands. Now he blanked his mind the way he always did. Reflex would guide his actions from here on.

With dreamlike slowness, the Mexican's right hand dipped down to the butt of his pistol. In the same instant, Tom clawed for his Colt. The weight of the gun seemed to slow the upward pull of his arm when his fist was filled with iron. He felt, rather than heard, the click of the hammer when his thumb jerked it back midway through the gun's sweep toward Valdez. Then he heard the concussion of a .44 cartridge, from beginning to end requiring less time than most men took to blink windblown dust from their eyes.

The roar of the gun faded, until there was only the

ringing in Tom's ears. Valdez had his pistol aimed at Tom, yet he seemed to be strangely frozen, incapable of pulling the trigger. Gunsmoke burned Tom's eyes but he dared not blink. Had he missed Valdez completely?

A spot of color below the Mexican's left eye caught Tom's attention, then Valdez took a step back and righted himself. His gun barrel wavered, just as a spout of crimson dribbled from the hole in his cheek to his shirt front. He staggered backward again and lowered his gun, his eyes rounded with surprise. Blood trickled into his beard, spreading, clinging to the ends of the hairs growing from his chin.

Tom let out the breath he was holding. Valdez was finished. Tom had been faster . . . he'd known it all along. His defeat at the hands of Luis Valdez was avenged.

Valdez let his pistol fall beside his right boot. He blinked and raised a hand to his face. Then his knees buckled. He sat down on his rump in the caliche and groaned. Blood coursed from his wound to his lap, tiny droplets making a splattering sound when they fell on his leather leggings.

Tom became aware of a noise coming from the far side of the river. It sounded like cheering, yet he couldn't take his eyes off the bullet hole in Valdez's cheek. He stood transfixed, gun still leveled on a dying man, as if the sight left him dumbstruck. It was a scene from his past, victory of a kind he'd known before. But there was something about this that was different. Absently, he wondered if it might only be the passage of so much time.

Onlookers were stirring in the crowd around them . . . Tom saw them advancing closer to the spot. All eyes were on Valdez, where he sat in a pool of blood, rocking gently back and forth with his hand pressed to his face to stem the flow of red.

Finally, Tom lowered his gun and started toward Valdez. His feet felt leaden, weighted down, as he crossed the thirty paces to stand over his adversary. When Tom's shadow fell over the Mexican's face, Valdez looked up, still wearing his silver-trimmed sombrero. The coppery scent of blood wrinkled Tom's nostrils. A knot tightened in his belly.

Still defiant, Valdez drew his lips across his teeth. *"El sol,"* he hissed. "The sun . . . was in my eyes . . ."

Tom knew it was a feeble excuse, for the sombrero kept out the sun. Valdez understood that he was dying, and still his pride would not allow him to accept the bitter defeat.

"I was faster," Tom said quietly.

"No!" Valdez protested, shaking his head, sprinkling drops of blood around him that looked like shiny new pennies in the sunlight. "It was . . . the sun!"

A groan whispered from his mouth, then his arms went slack and fell to his sides as he toppled over on his back, spilling the sombrero from his head when he fell. Now the sun shone down on his face. A tremor went down his legs, rattling one spur rowel. His arms quivered as a choking sound came from his throat.

Tom turned away. He had watched men die before. He saw Colonel Ortega riding slowly toward him, flanked by a pair of soldiers.

Ortega halted his horse. For a time, he stared down at Tom with pure hatred in his eyes. "Today, Señor Culpepper, you were faster," he said. "Perhaps on another day, Luis could have been first. It is the nature of things, the reason men gamble with their lives." He reached inside his tunic and took out Tom's envelope. "Here is the money." He tossed it on the ground near Tom's feet. "Take your cows and the horse, but heed my warning! Do not come back to Guerrero!"

He bent down to pick up the envelope. Crowds of curious bystanders were closing in around them. Turning on his heel, he started for his horse. The crowd parted to give him a wide berth on his way across the bluff.

When he was mounted, he looked over his shoulder at the crossing where splashing sounds echoed from the bank. Hank Wardlaw and Chap Grant were hurrying their horses toward the Mexican side, followed closely by Jesus Soto on his mustang pony. He waved to them and sent his bay toward the herd of longhorns grazing short grasses beside the river. Behind him, Hank and Chap and Jesus spurred to a lope to catch up to him before he reached the cows.

Hank was grinning when he came alongside Tom. "Fancy shootin', Tom," he said. "Let's get those beeves out of here before that Mexican has a change of heart."

Jesus slowed his pony when he caught up to the others. "The stallion!" he cried, pointing across the bluff.

Tom swung his bay toward the spot where the soldier held the stud. "Help Hank an' Chap get those cows across," he said. He'd almost forgotten about the white horse. "Don't waste any time gettin' it done."

He rode over to the Federale and leaned out of the saddle to take the stud's reins, noticing that the crowd had gathered around Valdez. Colonel Ortega was down from his horse near the gunman's body. It would have been a nice touch of showmanship to mount the stud for the ride back to Texas, but he decided against it. He had

245

everything he came for . . . his honor, the stolen cattle, and the Spanish Barb. Ortega wouldn't be the type to tolerate having salt rubbed in his wounds.

Leading the stud, he started back to the crossing, feeling better than he had in years.

Chapter Twenty-Two

Captain Hardin watched him ride out of the river. Deputy Cole sat quietly beside him. Tom rode over and handed the deputy the stud's reins. "That's my saddle," he said. "I'd be obliged if you'd toss it in the back of that wagon." He turned to Hardin. "I figure the horse is stolen, Cap'n," he went on. "I'm turnin' it over to you. Sooner or later, the owner will claim it. Somebody'll be lookin' for a good-bred stud like this when it came up missing."

Hardin nodded. "We'll see to it he gets back to his rightful owner. We'll post a few notices.

Tom was suddenly aware of the heat. He shouldered out of his coat and hung it from his saddle horn. The deputy had started to unsaddle the stallion, all the while looking up at Tom.

"That was the fastest draw I ever saw," Cole remarked around the plug of tobacco in his cheek. "I owe you an apology, Mr. Culpepper. You're a hell of a good hand with a six-gun."

Tom meant to ignore the compliment, reaching back to take the whiskey from his saddlebags. He could feel the stares of the people from Rio Blanco standing near the wagon when he pulled the cork and tipped the bottle to his mouth.

"You were mighty damn quick, T.C.," Hardin added. "Next time I see Captain Hollaman, I'll tell him he was dead wrong about you. I always believed age slows a man down when it comes to some things."

He saw Consuelo coming toward him. "This heat can be worse than a few extra years," he said, admiring Consuelo's curves. There was something about her yellow dress that made her look slimmer. "I've noticed hot weather seems to affect me more'n it used to." He swung down from the saddle when Consuelo arrived. While everyone was watching, he put his arms around her.

Hardin chuckled softly. "It don't appear the heat's botherin' you all that much, T.C. Not so's anybody'd notice."

Sheets of wind-driven rain pelted the roof. Thunder rumbled overhead. Spouts of water cascaded from the eaves, becoming tiny rivers across Tom's front yard. Puddles had formed in every low spot. Rain washed the sides of the adobes across Rio Blanco, turning the mud a darker color. Now and then, bolts of lightning brightened the dark sky. With the rain had come a clean, fresh smell. Tom stood on his porch inhaling the scent, watching the downpour. It had started to rain around midnight. By morning, the dry riverbed was flooded to its banks. A wry smile remained on Tom's face while the storm raged above him. "A man's gotta have faith in the seasons," he said aloud, though the sound of his voice was lost in a roll of thunder.

The dog looked up at him and wagged its tail. "Stop that infernal begging," Tom growled. "You won't get a scrap of food from my table until you've caught something on your own . . . like that damn rooster, for instance. This yard would be knee-deep in chicken shit by now if the rain hadn't come along to wash it off."

He ignored the whimper following his speech, otherwise occupied by rain-watching. In his mind's eye, he could see the grass growing across his pastures now. The dry spell had finally come to an end.

Quite unexpectedly, he saw a cowboy in an oilskin slicker trot his rain-soaked horse to the front of the cantina and climbed down to tie off his reins. "What sort of damn fool would be out in weather like this?" he asked. "I don't recognize him. Must be some gent from a ranch up north . . ."

The cowboy went inside the cantina. Tom studied the cowboy's horse for a brand he might recognize. A Rafter A glistened wetly on the sorrel's left flank. "Never heard of that outfit," he muttered. The stranger was just in time to be greeted by the stink of lye from Arturo's mop bucket. Tom knew that even if a foot of flood water ran through Arturo's cantina, he would still perform his daily mopping.

Moments later, the stranger reappeared in front of the cantina. He looked directly at Tom's house, then he went to his horse and got back in the saddle. Tom watched the cowboy ride through the puddles and the swirling rain. "Wonder what the hell this fools wants with me?" he asked himself, when the newcomer made for the porch.

The sorrel came to a halt a few yards from Tom. Raindrops pattered across the cowboy's slicker and the brim of his hat. He swung a leg over and stepped to the ground before he spoke. "Howdy," he said above the echo of distant thunder. "Mind if I come up where it's dry?"

"Suit yourself," Tom replied, puzzled by the stranger's arrival. He had a youthful face and wore a friendly expression, but it was Tom's nature to be suspicious of new arrivals in Rio Blanco.

The cowboy climbed the steps and offered his hand. "Bobby Sims," he said. "The feller at the cantina sent me over."

Tom took the handshake. "How's that?" he asked.

The stranger's eyes fell to Tom's gun. "I was just passin' through," he explained. "Hired on at the Rafter A for the fall roundup. The bossman gave us a few days off, on account of the rain. I asked one of the regular hands where the closest place might be where I could find . . . a woman, if you know what I mean. He told me there was this real pretty *señorita* who sold favors to cowboys down in Rio Blanco, so that's how come I'm here. The feller at the cantina told me that I'd find a woman by the name of Consuelo at this house. He said she used to live behind his place, only just recently, she'd moved."

Tom hooked his thumbs in his gunbelt and rocked back on his boot heels. "Consuelo don't take gentleman callers anymore," he said with some irritation. "She gave up the whorin' profession some time back. About a week ago, if I remember right. She's taken to reading scripture instead. You made a long ride for nothin'."

The young cowboy's face fell. "Just my luck," he

said, still eyeing Tom's gun. ''That Rafter A can be a lonesome place.'' He started to turn away.

''Next town with a whore is a day's ride,'' Tom advised. ''It'll be a rough ride in this storm. Our cantina has got decent whiskey and right good tequila. We've got a real pretty young woman in town too, but she sure as hell ain't no whore. Her name's Maria Flores, and so long as you're already here, you might pay her a social call.''

The boy's face lit up with a smile. ''You say her name is Maria Flores?''

Tom shook his head. ''But she ain't a whore, so you mind your manners around her.''

''Honest I will,'' he replied.

The sound of voices on the front porch brought Consuelo to the door. She peered out and smiled, passing a glance over the newcomer before she spoke to Tom. ''The food is ready,'' she said, then she closed the door.

Bobby Sims seemed anxious to be on his way to the cantina. He started down the steps. ''Thanks for tellin' me about the girl,'' he said, pausing, ''Mr . . . ?''

''Culpepper. Tell Maria that Tom Culpepper sent you over.''

Recognition widened the young cowboy's eyes. ''You're the gunfighter!'' he exclaimed. ''Word came to the ranch by way of a drummer that you'd won another gunfight over in Mexico!''

Tom was pleased that the boy knew his reputation. ''I reckon it was the fight with Valdez you heard about.''

Bobby's eyes clouded briefly. ''Don't recall the other feller's name offhand. But every cowboy at the Rafter A knew all about you, Mr. Culpepper. An old-timer by the name of Snuffy Weeks started to tell stories about all the gunslingers you'd faced. Snuffy claimed you are the fastest gun in all of Texas . . . maybe even the whole world.''

''That might me stretchin' it a bit,'' Tom remarked. The boy was carrying things a bit too far. ''Tell Maria I sent you, and be damn sure you conduct yourself like a gentleman, or you'll answer to me.''

''Yessir,'' the boy replied, with a last look at Tom's gun. He went down the steps into the rain and mounted his horse.

Tom watched the cowboy ride off, until the downpour was swept across the edge of the porch by a gust of wind. He backed away from the raindrops and started for the door, until a thought made him pause to look toward the Mexican border.

He had risked everything to reclaim his dignity. He had no regrets. Some men were made differently . . . honor had less importance. For Thomas Calvin Culpepper, it would have been a fate worse than death to live with the knowledge that he had shown any cowardice. Age had nothing to do with something like that. If he lived to see a hundred, he would feel the same way.

Until just then, he hadn't been aware that his hand was resting on the butt of his gun. He looked down at it and gave what would pass for a grin. He didn't give a damn what Delia Cummings had to say about it. He meant to wear his gunbelt until he drew his last breath. Some men were born to a gun, and if he had his way, he'd be buried with it tied around his waist.

A bolt of lightning coursed across the sky, illuminating the brushy flats below Rio Blanco, followed by a clap of rumbling thunder that seemed to shake the ground. Until the light faded, he could see silvery puddles between the dark outlines of spiny desert plants and the skeletonlike limbs of mesquites. South Texas would renew itself almost overnight, its thirst quenched by rains. Cows would fatten magically, ranchers would prosper. The four-year dry spell would be forgotten, and perhaps the town would start to grow again.

His gaze drifted to Rio Blanco. He wondered if a time might come when the town needed a sheriff again. "I could still do the job," he said quietly, then he opened the door and went inside, listening to the musical patter of raindrops on the roof.

THE ONLY ALTERNATIVE IS ANNIHILATION . . .

RICHARD P. HENRICK

BENEATH THE SILENT SEA (3167, $4.50)
The Red Dragon, Communist China's advanced ballistic missile-carrying submarine embarks on the most sinister mission in human history: to attack the U.S. and Soviet Union simultaneously. Soon, the Russian *Barkal,* with its planned attack on a single U.S. submarine is about unwittingly to aid in the destruction of all mankind!

COUNTERFORCE (3025, $4.50)
In the silent deep, the chase is on to save a world from destruction. A single Russian submarine moves on a silent and sinister course for American shores. The men aboard the U.S.S. *Triton* must search for and destroy the Soviet killer submarine as an unsuspecting world races for the apocalypse.

THE GOLDEN U-BOAT (3386, $4.95)
In the closing hours of World War II, a German U-boat sank below the North Sea carrying the Nazis' last hope to win the war. Now, a fugitive SS officer has salvaged the deadly cargo in an attempt to resurrect the Third Reich. As the USS *Cheyenne* passed through, its sonar picked up the hostile presence and another threat in the form of a Russian sub!

THE PHOENIX ODYSSEY (2858, $4.50)
All communications to the USS *Phoenix* suddenly and mysteriously vanish. Even the urgent message from the president cancelling the War Alert is not received and in six short hours the *Phoenix* will unleash its nuclear arsenal against the Russian mainland. . . .

SILENT WARRIORS (3026, $4.50)
The Red Star, Russia's newest, most technologically advanced submarine, outclasses anything in the U.S. fleet. But when the captain opens his sealed orders 24 hours early, he's staggered to read that he's to spearhead a massive nuclear first strike against the Americans!

Available wherever paperbacks are sold, or order direct from the Publisher. Send cover price plus 50¢ per copy for mailing and handling to Zebra Books, Dept. 4262, 475 Park Avenue South, New York, N.Y. 10016. Residents of New York and Tennessee must include sales tax. DO NOT SEND CASH. For a free Zebra/ Pinnacle catalog please write to the above address.